There was a flurry of movement as several more guests bid dear Helene Harpennis good night. Then, complaining that her devotion to duty to the Harpennis Foundation, to the ball, to the guests, et al, had prevented her from dining properly, darling Helene demanded a dish of the sorbet that had been served after the entrée. A waiter hastened away, returning almost immediately with a deep rose cassis ice. It was passed over heads and between bystanders from someone to someone, finally to Mrs. Harpennis. She dipped her spoon and ate.

As Margaret and Paul were leaving, they cast one look back before they turned to descend the stairs. Thus, with a long view of the room, they saw Helene Harpennis gasp, tense, and fall forward onto the table.

"   we investigate?" Margaret asked. "   hing seems to be wrong with Helene."

# SUDDENLY IN HER SORBET

## Joyce Christmas

FAWCETT GOLD MEDAL • NEW YORK

A Fawcett Gold Medal Book
Published by Ballantine Books
Copyright © 1988 by Joyce Christmas

All rights reserved under International and Pan-American Copyright Conventions. Published in the United States by Ballantine Books, a division of Random House, Inc., New York, and simultaneously in Canada by Random House of Canada Limited, Toronto.

Library of Congress Catalog Card Number: 88-91027

ISBN 0-449-13311-7

Printed in Canada

First Edition: June 1988
Fifth Printing: February 1992

*For my two titled friends:*
*Lady Joanna*
*and*
*Doctor Carole*

# Prologue to a Party

*It is* always a mistake to write the news in advance.

On a Thursday morning in mid-September, Poppy Dill sat at an antique typewriter in her ambitiously rose-colored boudoir and typed from notes written in her looping hand:

> *Get out your dancing shoes!*

She struck the exclamation point with pleasure. Poppy liked to splatter dramatic punctuation across her copy in a mistaken attempt to insinuate more excitement than actually existed into the events she reported in her daily society column.

> *The fall social season is off to a rousing start! New York's busiest fund-raiser and our favorite hostess is, as usual, leading the way. Legendary Helene Harpennis was at those grand doors of Harpennis House last night to greet each and every guest at her annual Harpennis Foundation Ball.*

While the Harpennis Ball would not occur until that evening, Poppy refused to admit that between now and then unimaginable disasters might come to pass: an aged legend could easily break a hip tottering down the marble stairway in her Charles Jourdan dancing slippers; a disgruntled social enemy might plant a bomb by those grand doors to demolish Helene and the first Excellency or Honorable she greeted.

When chided by her editor about this habit, Poppy Dill would narrow her eyes and remind him that she had been in the news business since before Brenda Frazier was the deb of her particular decade. The editor never failed to remind Poppy that Brenda Frazier happened fifty years ago, and in any case, what she wrote was not, strictly speaking, news.

> *More than three hundred admirers of Helene and Adjuvant Youth, the Harpennis Foundation's favorite charity, dined and danced to raise much-needed funds for underprivileged young people.*

Poppy had on numerous occasions extolled in her column the efforts of Adjuvant Youth to make this a Better World for the Deprived. Personally she was convinced that Adjuvant Youth was a collection of teenage thugs who had discovered a cunning way of not being tried as adults for their crimes.

> *The guests stayed till dawn, amid Basil Jones's divine pink and white decorations.*

Poppy saw this high-profile decorating job as a compensatory crumb Helene had tossed to Basil for services rendered. He had escorted Helene to a thousand fetes, fetched and carried for her for years, and worked tirelessly and unpaid for the foundation, although Poppy suspected Helene must subsidize him to some extent.

She consulted the guest list for the ball supplied to her exclusively by the Harpennis Foundation, and typed on:

*Among the revelers I saw . . .*

Here Poppy stopped. Suggesting that she had actually been in attendance was chancy. It was universally known that she no longer emerged from her East Side apartment for social events, not even for her dear friend Helene. Naturally there were the rare exceptions: invitations to meet selected members of the British royal family or the occasional first-rank celebrity, although now that Cary Grant was gone, there were few enough left. People came to her instead, as often as not bearing gifts, passing through her *faux marbre* foyer (a gift from decorator Morley Manton) to curry favor, to ensure a mention in her "Social Scene" column in the right context, or to prevent it in the wrong one. Poppy retained copious, locked files and a memory that stretched back half a century. She knew such affairs as the upcoming ball so intimately it didn't matter if she were there or not, so she wrote:

> *I saw Ambassador and Mrs. Dwight Duckworth, Morley Manton, today's finest interior designer, Helene's son Robert de Bouvet and his lovely wife Sara, who are visiting from their exquisite home outside Paris . . .*

Poppy expected to stay with the de Bouvets on her next trip to Europe.

> *. . . actress Jane Ackworth and the Honorable David Sears, Goneril Gmymth, Dr. and Mrs. Emil Glass, charming Lady Margaret Priam . . .*

Lady Margaret was so very well connected that it gave Poppy a special frisson of journalistic pleasure to mention her name. Dear Margaret really ought to marry again instead of flitting about with rich divorced men who paid too many ex-wives too much alimony. The polo players were even worse. They had to support their ponies.

> . . . *Leila Parkins (the busiest girl in our fashionable young set!), Count and Countess Hervé Cloissoné, she dressed by Givenchy as always, the Charles Starks, Prince Paul Castrocani. . .*

The prince was a new young face on the social scene, but the tides in New York Harbor washed up the flotsam of minor Continental aristocracy with boring regularity. In this case, Poppy was acquainted with his very wealthy American mother, now safely divorced from the impoverished (but delightful) Italian prince she had invested in back in the early sixties. From all reports, the son was as attractive as the father.

Poppy typed on, listing those possibly poor in spirit but rich in charity dollars, most of them eager to see their names mentioned in connection with a suitably exclusive event. Poppy's "Social Scene" column was never held up to journalism students as an example of riveting prose, but it served its purpose in being the only kind of newspaper publicity acceptable to the individuals named.

Friday's column was quickly finished. In addition to the coming evening's Harpennis Ball, it also detailed a showing of haute couture fashions the previous day that was notable for the number of socially prominent, leisured, and dangerously thin Manhattan ladies in attendance. The wrap-up story dealt with hitherto secret plans for a marriage that would unite an incredibly rich man with a brain reportedly the size of a pea and the woman who had been his previous wife's social secretary. The man in question had allowed Poppy to break the news in exchange for her keeping mum about a recent scandal that involved, in some combination, his son by an even earlier marriage, his bride-to-be, his horse trainer, and possibly some of his thoroughbred horses.

The copy was handed at noon to a messenger, who delivered it downtown to the newspaper's offices a good eight hours before Helene Harpennis took up her post at the doors of Harpennis House.

Poppy retired to her bed, propped up by plump satin pillows, to watch her favorite soap opera.

That sunny, golden September day in Manhattan, between Poppy's report of the news before the fact and the actual event, saw certain small occurrences related to the Harpennis Ball. None of them, of course, had any impact on the advance or decline of civilization as most New Yorkers know it.

A countess slapped her maid, called her lover, and finally chose the Givenchy she would wear to the ball. An aspiring Deb of the Century bounced a screaming fit off a satellite and across the Atlantic into her mother's ear, which happened to be located in a rented palazzo on the Grand Canal in Venice. She finally agreed to attend the Harpennis Ball after extracting a hefty price, above and beyond the income from her trust. When she hung up, she called a friend who had access to an unlimited supply of cocaine.

Several women who would attend the Harpennis Ball lunched together at Le Cirque on tiny salads. They smirked knowingly when they saw Helene Harpennis's daughter-in-law leave the restaurant and enter a pale gray stretch limousine with a man who was not her husband.

Those in charge of organizing the ball checked lists, counted cases of champagne, and prayed that not too many guests would pocket the silver flatware Mrs. Harpennis insisted on for tonight's dinner. The caterer would expect to be reimbursed for his losses and that reduced the amount that the foundation could announce had been contributed to Adjuvant Youth.

The man who had graciously been allowed to plan the ball decorations walked slowly through the high-ceilinged ballroom upstairs at Harpennis House for a final check of details. He had done an excellent job with the party decor —pink and white with a touch of deeper rose amid the silver—and he had overcharged the foundation for his services by a really tiny amount, out of pure friendship for dear Helene.

The overcharge was cleverly hidden among the figures in the account book tucked away in his desk in a corner of one of the foundation offices. What a relief that it was only a matter of time before he could forget such petty financial constraints.

Although he understood her reasons, he deeply, sadly regretted that the imposing mansion was no longer Helene's lavish abode. Built on Park Avenue by a turn-of-the-century railroad baron with wealth gouged from a grateful nation, it had subsequently been purchased by the late Nayland Harpennis, then turned over by his widow to the Harpennis Foundation. The foundation used it for its offices, as a site for charity fetes (some of them, regrettably, *not* top-drawer), and as a gallery to show the works of unrecognized and largely untalented artists.

He rested a moment in the lovely little library off the ballroom. If only, he thought, the house could have remained the epitome of old-world elegance, a private home to welcome visiting nobility, the cultured and the distinguished. A haven for Helene's devoted friends who lived only to please her. . . .

Helene's oldest friend stared out a window in the borough of Queens, from which she could see the splendor of the Manhattan skyline across the East River. She could remember sharing in the glow of other glittering nights orchestrated by Helene. So many of them, she thought, built on the strength of promises made and seldom kept. The rich and the aspirers to riches knew no loyalty except to themselves yet never failed to demand it from their followers.

Quite a few who thought of themselves as Helene's friends (but set limits to their devotion) had occasion to speak of her in the course of the day:

". . . and when she told my husband that she was *sure* she'd seen me on the Onassis yacht with . . . Well, it was decades ago, and it probably wasn't me at all, but I've never forgotten the terrible scene she caused."

"She's originally from someplace like Cincinnati—about a hundred years ago—but that's never bothered her."

"Good Lord, that noisy little woman who stayed with us in Scotland? A ball? Won't go. You shouldn't have accepted. What? You *paid*?"

"It's a gift, you know, finding the right person to marry, just when you need him. There was that Frenchman when she was stranded in Europe. And then old Nayland Harpennis, with his mountain of money. Fell for Helene utterly, and she wasn't terribly young. She must miss him, even if he did leave her the foundation to play with. One of these days she'll find another likely lad, even at her age."

". . . she was simply furious that time when Sylvia held her dinner the same night Helene was entertaining the ambassador. The best people went to Sylvia's because she'd snared Princess Margaret *and* Baryshnikov *and* Louise Nevelson *and* Malcolm Forbes. That didn't faze Helene. She simply packed up the guests who did show up at her dinner and took them all around to Sylvia's . . ."

"My mother claims she once spent two weeks thinking of tasteful ways to kill Helene. Years and years ago. It was something to do with Daddy."

# Chapter 1

$A$ *long* and active life, brimming with amusing contretemps and exhausting adventures, was slowly gaining on Helene Harpennis, but thanks to her astutely accumulated wealth, on this afternoon before her ball she still held the lead.

In seclusion in her huge Fifth Avenue apartment that had superseded inconvenient and drafty Harpennis House, Helene conserved her energy for the ball and lifted the receiver of a divan-side telephone.

"Basil darling, everything is in order for tonight." It was a statement, with the barest hint of query. "And the flowers will not wilt before the ball." She had had strong reservations about allowing an amateur like Basil to undertake the decorations, but he had begged. In any case, Morley Manton, who actually *was* an interior decorator, had declined on the spurious grounds that he was too busy.

She listened impatiently to a long statement from Basil that squeaked from the receiver. It caused an unfortunate little frown to appear; so bad for the aging forehead.

Interrupting, she said, "Naturally Janine Sheridan resents Nina Parlons being given so much responsibility for the ball this year, but I doubt *very much* that Janine would

8

presume to say anything like that about you, and certainly not about *me*." Helene's eyes narrowed. "I'll take care of it tonight when I see her." She hung up without a good-bye.

How tiresome to have these petty worries. Plots and counterplots. They wearied her as they would not have in the past. She hated to admit that she was beginning to feel her age. Not that she truly looked *old*, although the innocent bystander with a sharp eye would have no trouble observing the tiny lines, the papery skin, the gray under the artfully tinted hair.

Her maid, Claire, knocked gently and entered Helene's room to find her mistress reclining on her blue divan perusing the guest list for the ball through half glasses. Claire was one of the few allowed to see that concession to age, but faithful Claire would never tell.

"Madame, your tonic." Claire bore a tulip glass filled to the brim with a creamy liquid. She was a bony, middle-aged Swiss who had never been an adorable, rose-cheeked Heidi.

"Leave it for now," Helene said. "I suppose Robert and Sara are safely out?"

She expected her son, Robert de Bouvet, and his wife to fly over from France to attend her ball, but they would insist on staying with her, when she had so much to do, as though the Carlyle weren't good enough. Sara liked a free roof over her head, anyplace away from those unspeakable children of hers. And Robert—. Helene shook her head. He was well past forty, and still hopeless as a businessman. In that, so much like his father—may he rest in peace—but without the looks or charm.

Claire placed the glass on the gilt table beside Helene. "M. de Bouvet requested me to tell you that he has an appointment with Boggel Brothers. He said you would understand this."

Helene did. Dear Morley Manton had arranged for Robert to meet with one of the lesser wine importers to convince them that the de Bouvet estate wines were worth foisting off on the American public. They were certainly not favored in the sleepy French village of Bouvet-aux-Panaises where they were born. The villagers might tend the vines, harvest the grapes, and make the wine, but even they preferred to drink the wines of neighboring villages. There hadn't been a decent Bouvet-aux-Panaises since Helene had married into the de Bouvet family before the Second World War.

"Madame de Bouvet is . . . simply out."

Helene closed her eyes briefly but did not wince, preferring not to encourage lines between her brows. She did not wish to think what Sara might be up to.

"I have already spoken to Mr. Jones," Helene said. "But if Miss Parlons or Miss Sheridan call from Harpennis House . . ."

She glanced at her list, impatient with the names neatly typed by Nina Parlons. "Who *are* these people?"

"Please do not forget the tonic," Claire said, knowing how to respond to a rhetorical question when Madame asked one. It was one of her virtues, along with the ability to utter meaningful "umms" in counterpoint to Helene's highly colored recollections of lives that had flourished on several continents over a good many years. She was convinced that the haut monde, as represented by Madame, throve on a diet of verbal distortions designed to reflect positively on the teller, however terrible a light they cast on the subject.

"Madame should begin to prepare for the ball at three," Claire said. "That will allow me time to dress your hair."

"Fine, fine." Helene waved her away absently. The list engrossed her. At least in among the unknowns there were some people who mattered. People who had moved in and out of her circle for decades, in glorious salons, stately palaces, luxe hotels from here to the ends of the earth. Although she herself had in the dim, forgotten past begun as a nobody, her brilliant understanding of the value of well-planned marriages as well as less formal liaisons had placed her among the somebodies. Now she knew them all, and all there was to know about them.

She was glad to see Charlie Stark's name on the guest list, although she still didn't understand how he had come to terms with the fact that his present wife—so much younger—had once been an airline stewardess. And why should Dianne Stark imagine, with that background, that she had the slightest chance of being invited to chair the maxillofacial surgery benefit?

While she sipped her tonic, the remarkable Swiss formula that Claire had brought to her attention, Helene meditated on her Causes. Nayland's foundation, over which she now had sole control, wasn't quite what she hoped it would be. In large part, she thought, because Janine Sheridan as executive director was too drab, never daring. Nayland had trusted Janine and her unswerving (unhealthy, Helene called it) devotion to her job, but Nayland had been dead for more than four years.

She wondered, as she had frequently in recent weeks, whether Adjuvant Youth was quite living up to its promise. There had been one or two complaints about the group's activities that couldn't be readily excused by the fact that people apparently lived according to different rules in Spanish Harlem. Morley Manton dismissed the complaints as nothing—jealousy—but naturally he would. He had been among the first to urge Helene to fund the Youth's efforts to bring a little comfort into the sorry lives around them. She had come to believe he was less concerned about the poor unfortunates than he was tantalized by the aura of unknown danger that surrounded the boys and girls of Adjuvant Youth. What to do?

She had recently come across a rather distinguished and hitherto unpublicized disease that was sorely in need of research funds. She had even been approached informally about lending her name and giving her money. It was a hard decision—disease or poverty, the innocents blighted by pain or those blighted by the mischance of being born rather too dark and rather too far uptown to take advantage of the wonderful opportunities available in the vicinity of Bloomingdale's.

Her foundation trustees would not dare to argue with her when she decided on a change of charitable direction. The most independent one, an old friend of Nayland's, had conveniently just died. He had objected to the Youth, but Helene had prevailed. She intended to fill his place shortly with someone who would not defy her. But someone correct. Being a trustee of the Harpennis Foundation carried status. Too many thought they were worthy, but few had the right qualities. Helene was undecided about making the announcement tonight, after she had spoken privately to the one she had chosen—and those who believed they would be.

Her eye fell on a name crossed off her list. This would not do!

Helene picked up the receiver and dialed a string of numbers including the distressing area code that signified the party called did not live in Manhattan, but across the East River in Queens. Queens was a place one traveled through to get to the Concorde at Kennedy Airport, but it was not a place where one lived.

"Belle, dear. It's Helene. Your name has been crossed off the guest list for tonight. You promised . . ." She listened. The unfortunate little crease reappeared in her brow.

"You have never missed a ball. Your black dress is perfectly fine, and you have very pretty bits of jewelry. I insist that you come. Robert is here. You always want to see Robert."

Helene listened to excuses. Belle Nagy was one of those very old friends from whom Helene had extracted everything that friendship could demand and more. Belle, for her part, allowed her to and had since girlhood days when the one was a daring and delightful darling and the other was, well, simply Belle.

"Belle, if you told Janine Sheridan you wouldn't attend, she certainly did not tell me. And I do *not* imply that you went behind my back, but it does surprise me. You get out so seldom."

Helene believed that she had a responsibility to bring some pleasure into Belle's life. She didn't admit that since Belle knew almost everything there was to know about Helene, the pleasure she granted was very nearly a bribe for eternal silence.

"I won't hear a no," Helene said. "You'll find a very nice young woman at the door to bring you in, Nina Parlons, if I'm busy with my guests. Yes, Janine Sheridan will be there, but she's such a bore. No pizzazz. I thought the ball needed a bright new face."

Belle Nagy, on the Queens end of the line, had quite a lot to say that didn't please Helene.

"You're upset because I haven't set a date for the retrospective for Istvan?" Helene said. "You know I do want to honor his memory." Helene shuddered at the recollection of Belle's long-departed husband's gaudy daubings, of no definable school and of very little appeal or financial worth.

While Helene had married and remarried astutely, Belle had long ago—indeed fifty years ago—chosen to marry Istvan Nagy, a penniless if remarkably fascinating painter who was never kind to her, as Helene was aware, but apparently Belle was not, even now in her declining years.

For a variety of reasons, Helene tolerated Belle's fanatical devotion to her husband's memory, but her latest obsession—to have a retrospective of his paintings in the foundation gallery—made her almost willing to forget noblesse oblige and tell Belle not to bother to come to the ball.

"You know," Helene added gaily and untruthfully, "I have the trustees to answer to. Robert said *what*?" Helene's tone turned sharp. "He has nothing to say about my affairs."

At last, Helene took the line of least resistance. She needed tranquility, not this unseemly agitation.

"All right, Belle dear. We'll definitely decide about the retrospective tonight at the ball. Now you'll have to come. Yes, bring along the transparencies if you wish. Tonight, then."

Helen sighed at the soothing click when Belle hung up. Istvan Nagy forty and fifty years ago had been quite the man in most respects other than his art. As it was, Helene had managed never in all those years to let slip how attractive she had found Istvan, and further, that the attraction had been dangerously mutual. Belle was not a woman with a cosmopolitan approach to life and spouses, especially back then when they were all young, and Helene and Istvan were greedy for sensual delights and clandestine pleasures.

She lay back and sighed. It was so hard to remember after all these years whether she had truly been in love with any of the men with whom she had been so passionately involved. So many enchanting days and thrilling nights, so much devotion filled her past. But now she sensed devotion ebbing. Even Basil, who had pledged himself to her happiness (in return, to be sure, for certain little financial considerations and a place in society he would not otherwise have attained), had acquired entirely too grand a vision of himself. And there were the others: Janine Sheridan clinging desperately to her job at the foundation, Morley Manton's refusal to hear anything against the Youth, Robert and Sara behaving as though Nayland Harpennis's millions were theirs. Now Belle was being difficult. It was time to remind them all who was in charge.

She placed one more call.

"Darling Poppy, it's such fun, the ball and all. You'll give us a nice item in 'Social Scene'?" Helene was assured that all would be as she desired.

Poppy, with one eye on her giant television set upon which a soap opera couple lay entangled in expensive sheets, had a question.

"Marriage? I?" Helene could barely get the word out. "That is the most absurd... Whoever said...? Who could have implied...? I understand that you must check rumors, Poppy, but that is the most slanderous..." Helene was nearly speechless, a rare condition for her. "I have merely been thinking of naming the new trustee."

With a commercial break in the soap, Poppy was able to report another rumor that further inflamed Helene.

"I *may* have made a decision on the new trustee, but I have told no one," Helene said. "You'll be the very first to know—from me, not one of these presumptuous—"

In a rage that did not carry over the telephone wires to Poppy's boudoir, Helene could not think of a word to express her fury at those who passed on untrue gossip to the likes of Poppy Dill.

"Yes." Helene said too sweetly, "it will be one of the *really* good people."

The three hundred or so holders of two-hundred-and-fifty-dollar tickets to the Harpennis Ball did like to think of themselves as really good people, both for giving up a few dollars for charity and for, well, being "good" as opposed to being nobody to speak of.

Seventy-five percent of those attending did so because it was the better part of wisdom to stay within Helene's good graces. If she had no reason to think negatively of one, she had no reason to dredge up an old memory and utter her potentially damaging version. The balance were so undistinguished socially that Helen cared nothing about their sins or their virtues, as long as they paid the price of admission. At least half of the expected guests believed that Adjuvant Youth was a worthy, if somewhat obscure, cause that assisted those people (and apparently there were many) less fortunate than they. The rest didn't care.

Few of those scheduled to attend the ball were expecting a rousing good time. That was not part of the price of admission. Nevertheless, they all left boardrooms and hairdressers, afternoon trysts and Bergdorf's, in time to be home to change into evening clothes and ball gowns, to see and be seen by people they saw and were seen by two or three times a week under remarkably similar circumstances.

Only the ten lucky Adjuvant Youth whom Morley Manton had persuaded Helen to invite in an ill-conceived gesture of goodwill were truly looking forward to the evening. The five boys in the group lounged in the sun in front of the storefront "office" of Adjuvant Youth ("Help Your Brothers and Sisters, We Do") and discussed the possible advantages to be reaped in the midst of all that downtown money.

Eduardo Cruz mostly listened. Alone among the Youth, he was acquainted with the foundation people. Indeed, he had once met Helene Harpennis and had found her condescending and overbearing, although his actual description involved different words. The young ladies the Youth would escort laid aside faded jeans and leather and their lethal weapons to primp and curl for the occasion.

As the day wore on, it seemed more and more likely that Poppy Dill, in her dim boudoir, had lucked out again. The champagne chilled gently, ready to brighten the rouged cheeks of a hundred and fifty dazzling ladies and spot the starched chests of a hundred and fifty distinguished gentlemen.

\* \* \*

For Lady Margaret Priam, labeled "charming" by Poppy Dill and certainly that, as well as authentically aristocratic, attractive, and much in demand socially, the prospect of the Harpennis Ball carried mixed sentiments.

When Helene had urged her to come, she consented out of a sense of obligation. She had known Helene for years, since she was a child and Helene was a slightly raffish friend of her mother's. Helene after all had been kind when Margaret arrived on these strange shores a few years back. If nothing else, Margaret admired her brave efforts to achieve eminence in charity and society. It was a rough career, even for someone as single-minded as Helene Harpennis. The competition in New York was horrendous.

Although Margaret never lacked for escorts, she was presently without a man she cared about. There was always the remote chance that one of these charity affairs would cast up someone worth knowing, although usually the same old faces danced in and out, and one heard the same old gossip while one ate the usual second-rate food.

For this occasion, Margaret had not had to pry a free ticket from Helene, or to give up a precious piece of her modest private income to buy one, or even pay out funds from commissions earned from Bedros Kasparian. Kasparian, who employed her to fancy up his Madison Avenue oriental antique shop and lure in prospective customers who were looking for something pretty in a T'ang horse, had given her a ticket.

"I was a boy on the streets myself," Kasparian said when he handed her the ticket. "Filthy streets in places you never heard of, with Turks looking to skewer little boys with bayonets. So I bought a ticket for these Youth, but I don't like to be around the society people unless they are buying from me."

"How on earth did you get on the Harpennis Foundation mailing list? No offense, darling Kasparian, but you aren't a ball goer to my knowledge."

"Mrs. Harpennis once paid me a little too much for a jade Chi'en Lung table screen. Greenish-white, I remember, a nice piece. Genuine." He shrugged. "I suppose she remembered me." He studied the rug and added. "I confess that I knew her long ago when she was not quite as rich as she has become."

"No! Don't tell me you were one of her many rumored . . ."

Kasparian chuckled. "How flattering. She was quite the fascinator of men. Now she acquires clouds of piffling hangers-on. The one who was with her when she bought the screen, Basil Jones, tried to argue with me, claiming to have an eye for jade. All kinds of stones, gold, antiques, as well. Fancies himself a Renaissance man. Can't stand the type."

"Basil's not a bad sort," Margaret said absently. "Mild delusions of grandeur. A diligent dilettante who subsists on a small independent income, a little art criticism, and the kindness of strangers. I should say, on the kindness of Helene Harpennis. Are you sure this is Ming?" She was looking at a slim, carved ivory figure of a sage about nine inches tall, displayed in a backlit niche. "We have something like it at home in England. A military Priam was said to have stolen it during the sack of the Summer Palace in Peking. I never thought it was valuable."

"Aha." Kasparian said. "A little girl who dabbled in art studies at the Courtauld is questioning Kasparian about Ming? Naturally it's the real thing. Would Mrs. Harpennis like it?"

"Helene has become obsessed with good works, egged on by Basil, I suppose. He's the type to revel in these charity affairs that mimic society as he imagines it," Margaret said. "But I'll see what I can do."

"Good girl. You want to wear something from here? There's the pearl necklace I bought at the Sotheby auction. Modern of course, but very nice all the same." Kasparian beamed at her. Short, dapper, and bald, with a bristly white mustache, he did not look as though he had grown up on dangerous streets.

"I shall go unadorned," Margaret said. "Given what these women wear to charity balls, I shall stand out like a single rose among weeds."

Prince Paul Castrocani, not the least like a weed, but rather distinguished for one so young, spent the afternoon at a desk on which rested a computer terminal that he did not wholly understand, seven perfectly sharpened pencils, and a list of extensions so that he could quickly call any one of twenty young women also employed at United National Bank & Trust who were more than willing to save the bank's assets from his mistakes.

To his credit, he was uncomfortable with being totally unsuited to the position he occupied, a sort of fledgling international banker who did not grasp the relationship between the dollar and the yen, the pound, or the Deutsche Mark. His job was the result of a clever contrivance by his stepfather, Benton Hoopes, who wanted to keep Paul out of Texas, where he and Paul's mother lived, out of Europe's five-star hotels, where Paul preferred to live, and out of trouble.

Thus Paul had to work in New York City at an ill-paying job with an impressive description, while receiving an entirely inadequate allowance from his mother.

Born rich and Texan, she continued to be vastly wealthy in spite of her youthful marriage to Paul's father. After she and Prince Aldo Sforza di Castrocani had lived the good life across Europe for a time and had produced their own little prince, Carolyn Sue Dennis Castrocani had grown sick of the sight of olive groves and her husband's craving looks when a buxom blond Scandinavian tourist strolled by. She missed Texas barbecue. She missed Neiman-

Marcus. She did not, however, ever begrudge Prince Aldo the price of their marital adventure, which had been considerable.

Little Prince Paul was buffeted about from Rome to Dallas and back, invaded a Swiss boarding school not quite as exclusive or expensive as Le Rosey and left it, spent a hateful interlude at the University of Texas and several blissful years roaming the world's playgrounds on Carolyn Sue's money until his stepfather stopped the drain on his mother's funds.

"My assets are too intangible to survive here," Paul had complained long-distance to his mother upon arriving in New York. He could almost hear her herds of prime-beef cattle stampeding and her oil wells gushing as he spoke. "I am twenty-five years old, and I have no talents. I have a useless title, some social graces, I speak a few languages." Then he added hopefully, "I'd look even better with a tan. From the south of France."

Paul's mother was not moved. "Why, honey, you don't need damn-all anything else than what you've got. Look at your dear old daddy. He didn't have two lire to rub together and only that fancy name and looks to die over. He found me. You aim for a rich wife or at least a rich ol' girlfriend. The title alone is worth three, four times your allowance."

Paul would have preferred the multiplied allowance.

The glittering young partygoers, club dancers, café loungers, Aspen skiers, and habitués of the Hamptons he'd met in New York all seemed to have limitless funds, and he did not. It was expensive trying to locate a rich girlfriend.

He accepted invitations to dine out, preferably at those places where wealthy young women were in abundance. He shamelessly went to parties at which he knew no one but had been asked because of his title or because someone knew his mother. He had jumped at the chance to be a member of Helene Harpennis's Junior Committee for her ball because a free ticket came with it.

Paul Castrocani, tall, dark-eyed, sensuous—"a *real* prince" the bank's young women breathed to one another on their coffee breaks—stunned with a glowing smile the young woman who had joyfully run out to collect his beautifully tailored evening clothes from the dry cleaner. With enough Italian blood to assume that female adoration was his due, he passed through the longing glances of tellers and typists and out the bank's portals into the late afternoon.

The young women of United National Bank & Trust watched the tall, lithe prince depart with his dry cleaning over his shoulder, and their several fantasies do not bear recording.

# Chapter 2

*At eight* o'clock, the doors of Harpennis House were flung open. Couple by couple, the guests ascended the grand staircase and paused with practiced grace to show their best profiles to the society photographers. These lurked at the entrance to the ballroom to capture the appearance of the ladies on their way to dine and dance in extravagant gowns and many carats of jewels.

Lady Margaret Priam, in slinky, unadorned black, slipped through the barrage of flashbulbs unnoticed by the press but well noted by Helene Harpennis.

"Margaret, how delightful to see you." They brushed cheeks with care. "We *will* chat later. There's so much to do. Basil!"

Basil Jones, diamond studs aglow on his pouter-pigeon chest and frail strands of hair vainly attempting to recall the days when they covered his entire shiny scalp, kissed the hand of a countess and ignored Helene. She frowned for an instant as he darted away to upbraid a waiter serving champagne from a precariously balanced tray.

"He is good with details," Helene said, "but he is not in charge here. Ah, Dwight! Here is Lady Margaret for you to attend to!" And Margaret was carried off by Ambassador

Duckworth and his wife to go through the motions of another charity evening. She noted quickly that more amusing prospects were not immediately evident.

By ten, the assembled company had downed a number of cocktails and was well into dinner at the little round tables decorated with such care by Basil Jones.

Dianne Stark, her airline career notwithstanding, looked especially elegant as she leaned toward Prince Paul on her left and said, "What mad person has decided that *sauce d'oursins* is the flavor of the month? I've had it three times in the past two weeks. It does something peculiar to the taste of veal."

"Yes," Paul said politely. "Sea urchins are not my favorite taste, although I ate them often in Greece when they were recently deceased. That is, one murders them on one's plate."

"I see," Dianne said doubtfully. "Well, you know Greeks."

Paul nodded. He knew quite a number of Greeks, including the memorable daughter of one of the big shipping families. She had once forced him to roam frantically through the labyrinthine corridors of the Palace Hotel in St. Moritz seeking her room. He had never found it, thanks to the Palace's erratic room-numbering system, and had relieved his thwarted passions on the Cresta bobsled run instead.

Across the table from him, a Mrs. Nagy, not in the least stylish and certainly elderly and plain, ate her veal with a bemused expression. She was apparently not on the same party circuit as Dianne, so was unfamiliar with tonight's sauce. Mrs. Nagy had been introduced as Helene Harpennis's oldest and dearest friend but did not appear to be quite dear enough to be made much of by Mrs. Harpennis. Helene had passed by in a feverish round of the dinner tables, spoken a few words into Mrs. Nagy's ear, and vanished into the dim reaches of the ballroom. Belle Nagy gazed after the hostess of the Harpennis Ball with a tired little smile, then delved into the food placed before her.

"My youngest sister is coming to visit us from Rhode Island," Dianne said disingenuously, and Paul nodded warily. Escorting about an unknown and unattached sister was a steep price to pay for an invitation to eat dinner tonight at the Starks' table.

Sea urchins forgotten, Dianne dipped her spoon eagerly into the cassis sorbet the waiter was handing around.

"I think you and Susan would get along so well," Dianne said. "I'll have you around for dinner or drinks when she gets here, shall I?"

"By all means," Paul said. "Ah, I believe Mrs. Harpennis is waving at me. Will you excuse me for a moment?"

He was relieved to escape further discussion of the visiting sister, having been commandeered by Mrs. Harpennis to open the dancing with her, a singular honor for one so recently made a part of this inbred world. Paul managed to steer her unscathed through the crowd.

"A lovely dinner," Mrs. Harpennis was saying. "Nina did an excellent job. You've met Nina Parlons, I think? I barely had time for a bite, but I saw you were seated with the Starks and Belle Nagy. Such charming people, the Starks. And Belle is such a dear friend, *such* an interesting person, don't you think?"

"I didn't really have a chance to—"

"I wonder where Basil has got to. He was all over the place when I was trying to welcome my guests, and now, just when I finally need him . . ." Mrs. Harpennis kept up a steady stream of chatter that didn't need a response. She was so accustomed to years of autocratic chairmanship of committees for good and worthy causes that a dialogue, especially that her personal ball, was beyond her comprehension.

"As I was saying about your mother . . . such a charming

girl. One used to see her everywhere with the prince. He could be *quite* naughty, but one accepts that in Italians . . ."

Paul was fond of his father and did not consider him naughty, merely typical and enviable.

"Your mother used to come to Nice every year, and of course, one saw her in Rome . . . Sara, darling, your dress." This a sharp hiss to Sara de Bouvet, who danced by with a notorious womanizer. Sara had the slurred look that too much champagne engenders, and her emerald green gown was a trifle askew. ". . . and that delightful little accent. Southern, I believe?" Through her monologue, Mrs. Harpennis's eyes combed the room, making certain nothing more untoward was occurring at her ball than her daughter-in-law in slight disarray.

The table of Adjuvant Youth was quiet, its occupants possibly dazed by the whirl and the copious, unfamiliar champagne. They observed the dancers closely as one might watch the antics in an aquarium filled with exotic creatures who live and breathe in a totally different medium. The dancers in turn pointedly ignored the cluster of potential muggers in their midst. It was all very well to give money for charity, but one did not expect to have to associate with the recipients.

Lady Margaret nodded to the many she knew who danced by and was politely bored. Belle Nagy had timidly latched onto her as an old acquaintance. Margaret dimly recalled her from some tea party or gallery opening that Helene had sponsored.

"A lovely party," Belle said. "Lovely." She didn't sound terribly pleased about it.

"I am bored," Margaret murmured, mostly to herself but loud enough for Belle.

"Oh, Lady Margaret, you shouldn't be. Helene is the perfect, gracious hostess. So very kind."

Margaret looked around sharply.

"I remember many such lovely evenings," Belle said.

"Going back years. My husband and I . . . You know him, of course, or at least his work."

Margaret tried to recall a Mr. Nagy. He did not exist in her memory, nor did his "work."

"The artist," Belle said helpfully. "Istvan Nagy."

"Ah, of course." The well-bred lie slipped out easily.

"There will be a retrospective here soon," Belle said. "I'm arranging it with Helene. There will be so much to do. Hanging the show, attracting the best people."

"You ought to have Poppy Dill put an item in her column. She's fond of Helene's projects," Margaret said helpfully, but she was studying a woman dancing entwined with a man she had been seeing seriously only a couple of months ago.

"I've met her," Belle said. "Ah, there's Robert. I want a word with him. I've known him all his life. A lovely young man. You'll excuse me?" Belle was off to tug at Robert's sleeve.

Margaret knew both Robert and Sara de Bouvet and found them wanting. Robert was boring and unattractive—a disaster for a Frenchman. Sara was merely the daughter of a well-off American auto-parts manufacturer, who displayed her discontent with her marriage at every opportunity.

"Miss?" A tall Hispanic Adjuvant Youth had braved the scorn of his compatriots and was inviting Margaret to dance.

"Why, yes," she said, and found herself swept gracefully into the ball. The Youth was too intimidated to converse, so Margaret relaxed in the pleasure of the dance and scanned the crowd.

For a party of this size, there were remarkably few genuine eccentrics in evidence, only a number of women wearing gowns they could easily afford but should never have consented to wear. Clouds of expensive scent wafted through the room, and silky skin and perfect hair and the glint of diamonds set the style. There were many envious looks and haughty glances over bare shoulders as the women examined each other's hair, makeup, and costume and mentally framed ruthless assessments to be shared with their very dearest friends the next morning.

The perfect, gracious hostess glided past Margaret with the handsome young man Margaret knew from other affairs of this nature. Paul Castrocani, at least, was presentable, if ten years too young for Margaret. She decided to go home early, as soon as the Youth had released her from his grasp.

"... so delighted you consented to be our Junior Committee," Mrs. Harpennis was saying to Paul. "We like having young men—fortunate, well-bred young men—take an interest in the less privileged."

Paul did not disabuse her of her belief in his benevolence. He stopped listening and looked over her head—not difficult since she was barely five feet to his six—to search the ballroom for Leila Parkins, hands down the most luscious female at the ball. Indeed, Paul thought she was the most desirable young woman he had met in New York, and the very fact that he had failed to enthrall her made her all the more desirable.

Paul spotted Leila making her way across the room. Then the crowd of dancers blocked his line of sight, and he was again entangled in Helene Harpennis's words.

"... at the Palace in St. Moritz. I do dislike snow, but such a lovely group of people stay there ... Hello, hello, so glad you could come!" Mrs. Harpennis waved to a socially connected United States senator and his wife who had just arrived. Paul hadn't spent enough time in America recently to remember his name or state or party. No doubt he was a Republican.

Helene, dancing to a drummer different from the one in the four-piece band in front of the tall windows, caught Paul napping with a grace step. It was not a stumble. Even though she was not young, Helene was not unsteady. Moving fast in the dark, she was a glowing tribute to years of expensive care.

"Yes," Paul said. "The Palace is memorable. I used to stay there myself." And regretted that he was not there now.

He was distracted by the sight of Leila now sitting in bored conversation with Morley Manton, who did not care much for women per se but was unerring in recognizing a blossoming social bud when he saw one. They were excellent clients for his interior design firm, now and in years to come.

"I remember your mother as a little bride." Mrs. Harpennis's expression softened. "Such chic. I wondered how an American girl could manage it, and so young. Twenty-five years ago, it must be. Perhaps it was Gstaad. Do you ski?"

"I—" But Mrs. Harpennis expected no answer.

Leila was wearing something red that managed to cling precariously to the rise of her breasts. How does she do that? Paul wondered. But money can purchase state-of-the-art fashion technology far beyond the means of the lower orders.

"That beautiful, beautiful hair, swept up like two great black wings on either side of her face. I remember my husband remarking how lovely . . . that must have been de Bouvet, of course. The French do notice the *details* of a woman's looks."

Paul's mother, determinedly and intentionally blond from the time she emerged into some form of consciousness at the age of fourteen, was evidently not the woman Mrs. Harpennis was recalling so vividly.

"Sorry," Paul murmured, after Mrs. Harpennis made another grace step. He hoped he had not damaged her tiny, bejeweled foot.

"No." Mrs. Harpennis said firmly. "My mistake." The looping, shimmering feathers on her sequined evening hat bobbed. A member of an endangered species had died for Helene tonight. "Your mother was quite blond, of course."

"And remains so to this day."

"Indeed?" Mrs. Harpennis stopped dead on the dance floor and ignored the disastrous chain reaction set up among the dancers. A staid middle-aged couple were sent careening into a minor member of Scandinavian nobility. His partner, a Brazilian beauty who was rumored to have had her entire body lifted by Dr. Pitanguy, stumbled between the wives of the ambassador and the senator, who were exchanging innocent political gossip at the edge of the dance floor.

Showing animation for the first time, the Adjuvant Youth males scooped up the Brazilian lady and set her on her feet. They seemed reluctant to unhand her, and Paul expected the Adjuvant females to pull switchblades from their bodices to effect her release. Meanwhile, apologizing profusely to the Brazilian lady, the Scandinavian count managed to deliver a nearly lethal blow to the bare-to-the-waist back of a woman who had a vision of her body that was remote from reality.

Mrs. Harpennis was oblivious, so hard was she thinking about Paul's mother. "It was my impression," she finally said sternly, "that there was no longer a Princess Castrocani. I cannot be wrong about this."

So forceful was Mrs. Harpennis's conviction that Paul momentarily felt guilty that he was not an orphan.

"Let me think," she said. "I saw your father the year he lost all that money in the precious metals venture. I am positive that he said—so charming—that he was wifeless."

"My mother," Paul said carefully, "chose not to remain with my father after a certain point in their marriage. My father still lives in Italy." Where, Paul knew, the only precious metals (now or ever) he was involved with were a Bulgari watch given him by Paul's mother and the gilt on the frame of the alleged Raphael painting that hung in the family villa outside Rome.

"My mother is now Mrs. Benton Hoopes. She lives in Texas, whence she came."

"But of course! Carolyn Hoopes! I know her well." Mrs. Harpennis was delighted and danced with renewed gusto. "How could I have forgotten that she was your mother? Such chic! I always wonder how she manages it."

"Money is vital," Paul said with feeling.

Leila looked to be gathering herself up for an early departure, detained briefly by Dianne Stark, who might have wanted some pointers for her sister from Rhode Island on how to become a fashionable demitart.

Thankfully, the music stopped. Leila's expression of petulant boredom, which Paul found extremely seductive, remained. He thought he might waylay her at the door. Even though she had a well-known taste for professional athletes (although not, as rumored, exclusively black ones), on their rare encounters she had shown some interest in the fact that he was a real prince, in the way that Italian aristocracy are all real somethings or other.

"Paolo . . ." Paul winced at the sound of Basil Jones's voice. "Paolo and darling Helene! A perfect couple. The goddess of our little benefit and the dark-eyed prince leading the ceremonial dance."

If it were not that everyone knew Basil to be Helene's most loyal follower, Paul might have told him to cease and desist. Basil's presumption of familiarity irritated Paul greatly. It seemed to go back to a passing acquaintance with his parents in the remote past. However, the advantages of Helene's patronage outweighed irritation. So Paul nodded as cordially as he could manage, then noted that Helene had not responded to Basil with any noticeable warmth. She had grown suddenly tense and angry.

"Basil, I have needed to speak to you all evening. I had barely a *glimpse* of you, and you simply ignored me.

Where have you been? Have you been looking out for Belle as you promised?" She didn't wait for an answer, even though Basil nodded vigorously. "Basil, I am troubled. There are matters we must discuss before this evening is over. I have heard rumors I do not like. And there are other matters, serious ones."

Basil's expression of concern was convincing in its intensity. Mrs. Harpennis clung to Paul's arm, and he felt he could not disengage himself from her until the problem, whatever it might be, moved a step toward solution. Leila, at least, had not yet departed. She was now sitting down with the Adjuvant Youth. The girls eyed her warily, but the boys seemed to be enjoying her precariously contained breasts while calculating the resale possibilities of her gold jewelry.

"Basil, in the first place, there are people here who I am *sure* did not buy tickets."

"There are a few, of course, who are not quite . . . *us*, but you have to expect that. They all paid, I assure you."

"I have been observing, Basil." She spoke in a low voice and managed to keep smiling for the benefit of the crowd, but Paul felt her tense with anger. "I wish to have my ball and the foundation represent the finest, the *very* finest of their kind. I thought I could trust you and Janine. Now I find that I am wrong. I do not like a number of things I hear from third parties, Basil. You know what I refer to."

Basil grew pale before Paul's eyes. His confusion was clear. Paul realized that throughout their long dance, Mrs. Harpennis had contentedly chattered on, apparently without another thought in the world. But Helene was now incensed.

Basil sputtered and stuttered. "Who, what—? I saw no . . . The Youth are quite . . . Surely there's no cause . . . I have done nothing to . . . "

"Paul, my dear." Mrs. Harpennis looked grim. "Basil

and I must see about some foundation business. Basil, the Youth!"

Adjuvant Youth, spurred on by Leila, were beginning to mingle. It was impossible for the guests to ignore them now.

"But what can I do?" Basil looked terrified.

"You are among those responsible for them. And Morley. Where is he? They are his responsibility, too, although not for long. Come along," she said. "I will deal with them. They knew they were supposed to sit." She sounded as though her well-trained terriers had cast aside years of working obediently on and off the leash. "I simply don't know if it's worth the effort any more. Plots and counterplots, that's all I see. Find Janine. I might as well speak to her, too. Ah, there she is. Yellow is the worst color for her. She looks like a dead daffodil."

Mrs. Harpennis headed across the dance floor with Basil at her heels, the courtier distressed by his monarch's displeasure. Before they disappeared into the crowd, Mrs. Harpennis paused to speak a few words to the tall Youth. He shrugged and spread his palms as if to prove that he had not purloined a single diamond, gold bangle, or teeny tiny evening purse. Mrs. Harpennis forged on, gathering Janine and even Mrs. Nagy in her wake.

Although there was nothing he could pinpoint, Paul sensed that things were not going well. The genteel surface of the party was beginning to tarnish; the diamonds turning to paste. Not at all like the truly splendid entertainments he had attended in Roman palazzos and Bavarian castles in his much-regretted recent past.

He edged through the throng, exchanging a few words with those he had come to know casually during his brief time in New York. Sara de Bouvet had rearranged her clothing and was now at the side of her husband, although Robert de Bouvet did not look especially pleased about it.

He appeared to be urging her to follow in the direction of his mother.

Nina Parlons gave Paul a breathless hello. He had met her at the single meeting of the Junior Committee of which he was a member, and discovered she was not a wealthy and pretty young socialite but only the very pretty young woman who had organized the details of tonight's ball.

"It seems to be working out," Nina said, "but those Youth terrify me. Mrs. Harpennis and Mr. Manton both claim they do wonderful work among their peers in Harlem and places like that. I don't know, I think they're all drug dealers. Well . . ." She smiled up at Paul. "Only a few hours to go." She dashed away.

The dinner tables spread with pink damask held only a few nondancers. Leila had finally vanished. Morley Manton was alone, surveying the proceedings.

"Did you see Leila leave, Morley?"

"Ah, Paul. She's gone. Gone to slip out of her Scaasi into a down-and-dirty frock for serious dancing elsewhere. I think Scaasi is too mature for a child like Leila, but . . ." Morley shrugged. "They never take my advice when they're young. By the way, I'm having a few people over tomorrow for cocktails. You'd like them. They'd love you."

"Sorry, I'm booked," Paul lied. He had gone to one of Morley's intimate gatherings where some quite bizarre men had propositioned him, some rather peculiar women had discussed artists, psychiatrists, and sexual positions with which he was not familiar, and the relentless white, chrome, and mirrored decor had disoriented him. He had made his escape after the sushi was passed around for the second time.

"Another time," Morley said. "Or if you get unbooked, give me a call. By the way, what seems to be troubling Madame?"

Paul shook his head. "Something about Basil and the

Youth. I believe your name was mentioned."

"Aha!" Morley stood up. He was extremely tall, beautifully dressed, and infinitely superior. He knew Important People. "We can't have that. Ciao." He caught up with the Harpennis parade that was making its way through a door at the end of the ballroom.

Paul headed for the curving grand staircase that led from the second floor to the equally grand marble hallway where the coatroom had been established. He was in time to see Leila's back as she swept out the front door. She had picked up Prince Gustav von und zu Lehrenmacht and Cummings Black III en route, the way dust is attracted to a television set.

"It's a pity," a voice behind him said. "The flame sometimes moves too fast for the moth. You'll have to live to die another day."

Lady Margaret Priam, wrapped in a flowing mink, was amused.

"Hello, Margaret. I caught a glimpse of you upstairs."

They had met on similar occasions and had chatted politely over a glass of champagne and a toast round topped with a dab of caviar about mutual acquaintances in many countries, the traffic in Rome, the best pubs in London, the crowds at Marbella. There is an instant affinity between Old World aliens of a certain class meeting by chance in New World marble halls.

Paul glanced again at the heavy front door, gleaming with brass and firmly closed behind Leila.

"She's so very rich," he said wistfully.

"And young and pretty. A combination to be envied by those of us who have slipped from grace in such respects."

"You exaggerate, Margaret." Paul knew she was only about ten years older than he, perhaps in her mid-thirties. And while she might not be all the things Leila appeared to be, she was a good-looking woman from a venerable Brit-

ish family and must have sufficient funds to keep herself
well.

"Come, love, let's go somewhere and have a drink,
away from all these benevolent folk. I loathe benefits."
Margaret linked arms with him.

"And leave your escort behind?" Paul feared to offend
some socially impeccable, well-off gentleman who banked
with United National Bank & Trust.

"I came alone tonight," Margaret said. "Dear old Kasparian, the man I work for, gave me a ticket. I certainly
wouldn't hand over two hundred and fifty hard-earned dollars to ensure myself a tedious dinner companion. I can get
that for nothing."

"I didn't know you worked." The idea that he was not
alone in the bonds of wage slavery in Manhattan made
Margaret all the more appealing. Since he had lost Leila to
the lure of the downtown clubs, an hour or two with Margaret seemed more interesting than going home early and
alone.

"Naturally I work. It's part of nature's plan. Work, get
money, eat, live. My siblings have never grasped that, so
I'm the only member of the family to seek American
streets paved with gold. While they dribble away their cap-
ital, I try to live almost within my means—with as much
style as I can manage. You do understand."

"Quite well. I ought to say good-bye to Mrs. Harpennis," he said. "She knows my mother. . . . "

"She knows everyone's mother, including mine. In fact,
due to some romantic entanglement with somebody in my
family quite a few years ago, I've always thought of her as
sort of a relative."

"She might be useful to me."

"Only in relation to how useful you are to her. But
you're young, white, single, a prince, and she'll probably
overlook the Italian part, so you're already useful for filling space at her benefits. I'll come with you. I tried to

catch up with her when I was leaving, but she appeared to be off on a tear. I've never known her to lose her temper in public. It isn't done. But I suppose these balls are a trial to put together."

They ascended the staircase, arm in arm.

Although some guests, like Leila, had reached their toleration level and departed, the ball continued in full swing and with as much lively abandon as very senior law partners, bemedaled diplomats, and habitués of European rejuvenation clinics could muster.

The Adjuvant Youth were demonstrating to the ladies and gentlemen of the Social Register the finer points of dancing. Someone had bribed or threatened the band to play some vaguely Latin music.

Margaret and Paul paused at the top of the stairs and saw a tableau of Helene and her minions, seated now at a distant table. Belle Nagy leaned solicitously over her shoulder, fluttering a handkerchief. Basil mopped his brow, his face as pink as his damask tablecloths. Sara and Robert sulked near the table, while Janine wrung her hands. Morley sat beside Helene, the better to eavesdrop, while Nina hung back as though she found all of it distasteful. Dancers who hurled themselves in their direction stopped to speak to Helene, bent to kiss her cheek, and swirled back onto the dance floor. After initial confusion, it now seemed to make no difference to the dancers that the band was attempting a lively samba. The Brazilian lady was dancing with four of the Youth, injecting a vigorous dose of Rio into the proceedings.

Here it became confusing. Mrs. Harpennis, no doubt complaining that her devotion to duty to the Harpennis Foundation, to the ball, to Adjuvant Youth, and to the guests had prevented her from dining properly, demanded a dish of the sorbet that had been served after the entrée. There was a flurry of movement that included several more guests who had come to bid her good night. A waiter hastened away, dispatched downstairs to the kitchens; the group around Helene ebbed and flowed. A waiter returned bearing a tray. The deep rose cassis sorbet was passed over heads and between bystanders from someone to someone to Mrs. Harpennis; a spoon was handed to her. She dipped the spoon, she ate.

"She's not in any mood for interruptions," Margaret said. "I'll send round a note in the morning. You do the same and praise it all effusively. She'll invite you someplace soon."

Margaret and Paul cast one look back before they turned to descend the stairs. Thus they had a long view of the room and saw, but did not register, that Helene Harpennis gasped, tensed, and fell forward onto the table.

For a moment, Paul didn't understand the commotion that arose, the voices raised shrilly above the music, people craning to see the cause of the disturbance. Then the music ceased abruptly in mid-phrase.

"Hey, man." The unmistakable voice of the ghetto issued from an Adjuvant Youth, but events had superseded the possibility of dance.

"Shall we investigate?" Margaret said. "Something seems to be wrong with Helene."

"I think we should not." Paul was thinking quick getaway, but Margaret grasped his arm firmly.

It was not so simple to move ahead. A whirl of color surrounded Helen's table as everyone pushed and gaped at whatever was occurring. Quickly a few of the more perceptive guests eased away toward the exit. Then a tide of guests surged toward the stairs, like panicked sheep hurtling toward freedom. Margaret grabbed the arm of a slim, white-jacketed waiter.

"What happened?" The tones of one accustomed to expect an answer from a servant worked admirably. The waiter halted.

"The lady fell right over onto the table. I think she's . . .

she's dead. The doctor told me to call an ambulance and say it was a poisoning."

He raced down the stairs, brushing aside those hurrying to depart before the cloud of scandal descended. Basil pushed his way through toward the staircase, moving as quickly as he had ever moved in his petite patent-leather evening shoes.

"Phone in the office," he panted. "Ambulance . . ." He fled down the stairs.

Janine Sheridan followed, looking terrified. "I don't know what . . . I just don't know . . . A Dr. Mittman is here. The Dr. Emil Glass who came tonight turns out to be a dentist."

"Dead, I'm sure of it," Charles Stark was overheard saying to the well-known symphony conductor who had attended in the hopes of interesting Mrs. Harpennis in making up his orchestra's deficit. "The end of an era. Like the burning of the library at Alexandria. The knowledge of centuries gone. Helene knew everyone."

"And everything," the conductor said. "To the peril of some."

Janine seemed to be in shock. Strands of graying hair had loosened themselves from the proper bun at the nape of her neck, and the rosy blush she had applied to her cheeks stood out harshly against her pale skin. Her mouth moved, but she made no sounds. Basil panted back up the stairs against the flow.

"I called," he said. "It never should have happened. How could it?" He was wringing his plump, bejeweled hands.

"What exactly did happen?" Again Margaret used the voice of command.

"Don't know. I have to get back," Basil said.

Margaret laid a hand on his arm.

"Janine says a doctor is with her. Tell us."

"I had been discussing foundation business with her in

private, in the little library off the ballroom. It might have waited, I don't know why she had to spoil my evening with business." Basil seemed close to tears. "I left her, Mrs. Nagy wanted to speak to her."

Janine interrupted. "She wanted to see me, too, privately, and then Morley. Then she came back into the ballroom and sat down . . ."

"And asked for a dish of that lovely sorbet served at dinner. People were stopping to speak to her."

"A waiter brought it."

"She took one bite."

"Fell forward right into it."

"She's dead, I know she is." Basil moaned.

"You don't know she's dead," Margaret said. "We'll have to find out. Come along, Paul."

In spite of very strong reservations about getting involved, Paul followed her through the few remaining patrons of charity. The Adjuvant Youth had disappeared totally, without passing them on the stairs. No doubt they had cased the mansion earlier for a convenient quick exit.

Margaret and Paul found that Helene Harpennis was indisputably dead.

## Chapter 3

"*It must* have been a heart attack," Paul said. He hoped it was and suspected it wasn't.

Someone had commandeered a pleasant coromandel screen from the little library off the ballroom and placed it so as to shield from prying eyes the table at which Mrs. Harpennis had gone to the great ballroom in the sky.

"Helene's heart was all right," Margaret said, "and she would regret the dollars lost this evening toward making a better world. I believe they were supposed to extract some many thousands of dollars from befuddled attendees by auctioning off a perfectly dreadful fox coat. I saw it." Margaret pulled up the collar of her mink, implying that there are furs and then there are furs.

The ballroom was now nearly deserted, so quickly had Helene's dear friends departed in the wake of the unexpected and the distasteful. The musicians were stowing their instruments and sharing a joke. They were accustomed to early closings due to unforeseen circumstances. Empty of guests, with the flattering candles snuffed and the overhead lights on, the ballroom with its ravished tables and unfinished glasses of champagne going flat looked like an abandoned movie set.

Margaret led the way to where Basil and Janine sat in stunned silence. Nina stood beside them. She smiled weakly at Paul. Far off by herself, Belle Nagy fumbled in her purse and wiped a tear.

"Do you have any idea exactly what has happened?" Margaret asked. "Is she dead?"

Basil and Janine were mute. Then Basil moaned. Janine nodded and gestured toward the screen.

"We don't know what happened," Nina said. "But I think . . . I'm sure she's dead. It was awful, so sudden. Nothing we could do." She looked to be on the verge of tears. "This isn't going to be very good for my career as a party organizer."

Paul put his arm around her shoulders, and she brightened considerably. "It wasn't your fault," he said. "It could happen to anyone. I mean, accidents happen."

"You can't imagine what these catty women will say," Nina said. "The doctor is there with her. Would you . . . ?"

Nothing could have kept Margaret away, and since she grabbed his hand and pulled him along, nothing hindered Paul. They peered around the screen.

A short, bald man in well-tailored evening clothes stood with his hands behind his back, contemplating the rigid form sprawled on the table, decorously covered with one of Basil's pink damask tablecloths. He turned abruptly to Margaret and Paul.

"And you would be?"

"A member of the family," Margaret said without hesitation. Paul admired that. An Italian might have decided first who wanted to know, what it might cost if he told, and whether it would be wisest to prove conclusively that he had been visiting relatives in Milan for the entire week.

"Mrs. Harpennis is . . . was . . . an aunt," Margaret said. "We were very close."

"Surely not closer than the son." The doctor eyed Margaret suspiciously.

"Well, no. Not that close."

"In any case, the son is having an attack of hysterics. I do not like to see that in a grown man. And his wife appears to have chosen the path of least resistance."

"She passed out," Paul said.

"Very astute, young man. Now, I am Dr. I. S. Mittman. I was asked to come to this lady's aid, although it was not my intention to practice my profession here tonight. There was no aid possible, I am sorry to say. I instructed one of the waiters to summon the police and an ambulance. I have nothing further to add, and I believe that you two should not be here. Presumably everyone, except myself since I know I did not perpetrate this horror, is a suspect."

"She was actually *murdered*?" Then Margaret sniffed, and smelled a heavy almond odor.

Dr. Mittman said, "It seems unlikely that the caterer for this evening could err so grossly as to place cyanide in one serving of the sorbet." He shrugged. "But I may be wrong. I understand from my wife that trustworthy help is difficult to find nowadays. There is a language barrier, she tells me."

"Doctor, this is serious."

Dr. Mittman pondered this, as though he were puzzled as to whether she was referring to the murder or the servant problem.

"I mean," Margaret added, "if people like Helene Harpennis get murdered, why then . . ."

"No one is safe?" Dr. Mittman smiled faintly. "Don't worry. I believe this sort of thing is comparatively rare."

"I think we ought to leave," Paul said. He did not approve of light conversation in the presence of death, especially that of a person he had been dancing with a short time before.

"Perhaps you should stay," Dr. Mittman said. "Did I hear whom you two are?"

"Lady Margaret Priam," she said, very aristocratic now.

"And this is Prince Paul Sforza di Castrocani."

"A veritable House of Lords," Dr. Mittman said. "I think I would ask you to stay until the police arrive. I don't wish to be abandoned by all sensible people, since my wife has gone home. Not that I mean to imply a great burden of sense there, as she chose to attend this evening's affair. They"—he waved a pudgy hand in the direction of Basil, Janine, and Nina—"they seem to serve some function in the organization that produced the festivities but are unwilling or unable to be of assistance. Perhaps one of them is responsible. Similarly the others . . ." The thin wail of an ambulance siren penetrated from the outside.

"At last," Dr. Mittman said, "the ambulance and, if I am not mistaken, the police."

Two uniformed New York cops appeared and stopped at the door, too late to halt the flight of society but soon enough to prevent the distraught mourners from fleeing as well. A youngish man in a windbreaker and jeans strolled in and paused to take in the after-the-ball debris. The man in the windbreaker proceeded toward the doctor and the pink-draped form that had been Helene Harpennis.

"I am De Vere," the man said. "The police."

He flipped open a scruffy leather folder showing a shield and identification.

He looked at the three of them. "And you are . . .?"

Paul, Margaret, and Dr. Mittman deferred to each other with the grace of long social experience.

"I want to know who you are," De Vere said, "not who gets to lead the way into the banquet hall."

"Lady Margaret Priam."

De Vere winced.

"Dr. I. S. Mittman. This is not really . . . my field."

"No? I suppose not many doctors specialize in death. On purpose, I mean. And you?"

"Paul Castrocani."

"That's it? No title, no identifying preliminary?"

"Well, of course he has." Margaret was looking at Detective De Vere as though she liked what she saw: a man with humorous brown eyes in a pleasant if imperfect face, a lean, well-kept body, and an unreadable, detached expression. "He's . . ."

"Paul Castrocani," Paul said louder.

"A prince," Margaret added quickly.

"And a gentleman and a scholar as well, I don't doubt," De Vere said, "A prince, heh?" He turned to the doctor. "I assume that the information I received is correct. A lady is dead. Circumstances unexplained."

"Correct to a point," Dr. Mittman said. "There is an obvious explanation as to cause, although I don't wish to commit myself."

De Vere lifted the edge of the pink tablecloth. "Ah." He sniffed and dropped the cloth. "Cyanide? Have these people no imagination?"

"Cyanide appears to be correct," Doctor Mittman said. "As for imagination, I have not detected a great deal in the group that was present tonight, but I do not know them well. Perhaps under different conditions they are brimming with imagination. The lady was dead before I reached her. If it was cyanide, it happened very quickly, presumably respiratory failure. There was no opportunity for resuscitation or other measures. Well, I am speculating here. I came to her aid, and there was no aid to be given."

"I see," De Vere said. "The medical examiner is on his way. Who might the deceased be?"

"Helene Harpennis," Margaret said. "I've known her for years, and she was sort of a distant . . . kinswoman. She's the head—indeed, the heart and soul—of the Harpennis Foundation, which gives money to worthy causes. She was interested in the Adjuvant Youth. They are—"

"I know who they are," De Vere said. He turned to the doctor. "I suppose everyone messed around the table."

"I tried to keep people away when I reached her," Dr.

Mittman said. "Not easily done. They were shocked and upset, and they do not . . . take orders readily, being more accustomed to giving them."

Several more blue uniforms had appeared at the door.

"Who did it?" Detective De Vere asked the question as though it were a matter of idle curiosity, the way one asks who is doing the maintenance on one's Jag these days, or who is one's current hairstylist.

There was quite a long pause while the three of them tried to come up with an answer. Dr. Mittman had the first, and the best, response. "If I knew, I'd be home by now. The way everybody else went home, taking their secrets with them."

"I couldn't begin to guess," Paul said.

Margaret said, "Assuming it was not something like suicide, which is unlikely if you knew Helene, or a terrible accident, then any one of the three hundred people who were here tonight could have done it. No, I exaggerate. Some people were quite fond of Helene, but naturally there were strong feelings. She tended to gossip—love affairs, big and little quarrels, secrets of the past. And the foundation gives away a good deal of money, I believe. I suppose money is always a motive for rash deeds. Helene had a lot of money. Then there's status. I don't know if that conveys much to you, but in this world . . ."

De Vere rubbed his forehead. "Let me rephrase the question."

They looked at him expectantly.

"Who did it?"

"Don't know." They spoke as one.

"Thank you." De Vere surveyed the others. "What about them?"

"They're all involved with the foundation and the ball and Helene in various capacities," Margaret said. Helene's minions were beginning to look both scared and wilted. "I don't know that they know anything more than we do, although they were all close by when it happened. Paul and I were more or less leaving and only saw the final moment from across the room. But I could be wrong. I am quite often wrong."

"Not, I'm certain, about things that matter." De Vere actually grinned. "I'll speak to them next. Is there any reason why you two stayed—other than Lady Margaret's distant kinship?"

"We weren't returning to the scene of our crime," Margaret said. "Truly. We came to see what the trouble was, bucked the tide, actually, since everyone else couldn't wait to get away."

"I asked them to remain since they were not behaving irrationally," Dr. Mittman said. "Not the case with the deceased's son, who is in the library over there highly discomposed, along with his wife and one or two prying friends. I would like to leave now. I can be reached at any time."

"Go," De Vere said. "But speak to the medical examiner first. He just arrived." He indicated a harassed-looking man who was making his way toward them. The ballroom was beginning to fill up with photographers and serious, official-looking men.

Dr. Mittman brightened at the sight of the other doctor. "Harry! It's been years."

"Irv." The medical examiner spread his arms wide. "It's been twenty years. Thirty. You're looking good. So tell me what this is about."

The two doctors went to inspect the body.

"I have always known there were more Old Boy networks than this world dreams of," De Vere said, half to himself. He turned to Margaret. "What about the other people here tonight? You know them?"

"Most of them. By name at least. The foundation would have a list of the guests."

"Is there a number where you two can be reached tomorrow? Later today, that is. I don't know whether it will be necessary, but since you saw it happen . . ."

"We didn't actually see anything," Paul said quickly. "Not that I am not glad to be of help." Police made the European half of him nervous; in his experience, they were not respecters of class distinctions. Not that De Vere resembled any police figure he had ever encountered. Paul liked his looks—world-weary, cynical, but conveying substantial authority behind the casual front.

"Paul will be at my place for lunch tomorrow about one," Margaret said, and gave him a warning look when he was about to say something. "It's a long-standing tradition we have." Margaret smiled prettily at De Vere.

"For years," Paul said. He hoped that Margaret wasn't going to involve him in the messy aftermath of Helene Harpennis's death. At all costs, he must not get involved with the police. Benton Hoopes would not like it, and he was capable of relocating Paul to a bank in Wichita if he chose.

"Here's my number." Margaret handed De Vere a card.

"Good. I'll tell whoever is assigned to the case where to find you."

"You won't be assigned?" Margaret said, disappointed.

"Unlikely," De Vere said. "I'm in a different department. I happened to be handy tonight." He smiled genuinely at her. "But I'll tell whoever it is to mention my name. As I said, networks are important. You . . . Prince . . . I'd better have a number for you too."

Reluctantly Paul gave him his number at the bank.

"May we leave now?" Margaret became haughty and very British. Paul thought that it must be that Detective De Vere had caught her fancy, but now that he wouldn't be involved in the case, she was no longer interested.

"Certainly," De Vere said. "I was only keeping you around because I like the way you look. Aren't you hot in that coat?"

"One never is," Lady Margaret Priam said. "Come, Paul."

As they reached the door, De Vere was lining up the others on one side of the room. Janine seemed ready to faint. So did Basil. Paul caught sight of Morley Manton peering from the library. De Vere commanded him to join the group.

At a question from De Vere, Basil gestured to demonstrate what had happened, and the others nodded their agreement.

Dr. Mittman joined Margaret and Paul at the staircase.

"A bad business," he said. "I wouldn't have taken the people here tonight as murderous, except perhaps for that group I understood to be the Adjuvant Youth. I should imagine that they would choose a more direct method than poison, however. They did not appear that subtle. Well, my dear Lady Margaret and . . . um . . . Prince, it has been a more unusual evening than I bargained for. In the future, I shall send my charitable contributions directly to the users and bypass the mayhem."

Dr. Mittman walked off briskly down Park Avenue.

By mutual consent, Margaret and Paul did not discuss the evening while riding in the taxi that dropped Margaret at her Upper East Side apartment.

"We'll talk all this over tomorrow," Margaret said as Paul helped her from the cab.

"I don't know if I can get away." Paul said. "The bank isn't keen on instant traditions."

"Do try, please. Make up a story. Claim Helene as an aunt, too. She was entangled with enough families here and abroad to make it not impossible. Come to think of it, I heard that she was your father's mistress years ago."

"I think she would have been too old for him. More likely my grandfather's. The old principe had a reputation for enticing wenches into the vineyards. I suppose I can 'help the police with their enquiries,' but United National isn't going to like it."

He walked her into the ornate lobby of her building. Even in these small hours, an army of uniformed doormen lurked among the marble columns and behind the sprightly potted trees. No unwanted foot ever trod those expansive halls; no uncouth members of the lower orders paused to admire themselves in the gilt-edged mirrors. Margaret had clearly chosen to apportion some of her inherited resources to suitable housing.

Paul walked with her to the bank of elevators.

"Who do you suppose . . . ?" he began.

"Did it? Can't imagine. Helene could be imperious and irritating and insulting, and even stupid, but murder is an extreme revenge."

The elevator was descending slowly, the lights of the floors winking on and off as it came toward earth.

"Was she always so . . . changeable?" Paul asked. "She talked on and on about my mother—quite inaccurately— and about St. Moritz and skiing, but when Basil came to us, she was a different person. Very angry. I did not expect this."

"No," Margaret said slowly. "She wouldn't normally behave that way at all. The facade was very important to her—the look of things, rather than the reality. Always the great, gracious lady, no matter what she was thinking or feeling, no matter how she browbeat one behind the scenes. But that's the way it often is with people like Helene who had to struggle up the social mountain. There are always things to hide."

"She did not seem pleased with anyone tonight," Paul said. "I wonder what Basil could have done to anger her so."

"Basil is pretty silly, a lot of pretensions and not much money, but always devoted to Helene. What I wonder is what Helene could have done to anger someone enough to murder her. The police are going to have a hell of a time getting straight answers from that crowd. We may never know who did it."

The elevator arrived and slid open with expensive silence.

"I wonder," she said slowly.

"Wonder what?"

Margaret grinned. "I wonder what department Mr. De Vere really is in. Night, love."

The elevator door slithered closed behind her.

*Chapter 4*

### SOCIALITE MYSTERY DEATH
### AS BAND PLAYS ON FOR CHARITY

Helene Harpennis had achieved the dubious recognition of a *New York Post* headline.

Curled up on her big chintz sofa the morning after, with all of Friday's papers around her, Margaret felt sure she would never achieve in life or in death anything that would warrant the *Post*'s front page. Even on a slow news day.

The story was necessarily brief, squeezed into a hastily remade page to make the early edition. The facts were egregiously wrong. Helene had certainly not been eighty, although Margaret would bet that was only about five years on the high side. Her husbands were noted: Henri de Bouvet (divorced, now deceased), and Nayland Harpennis (deceased), plus a youthful marriage to no one of any redeeming social value. (That one was rumored in Helene's circles to have been a teenage elopement, soon dissolved, that had removed her from the Midwest and started her eastward to Manhattan and Europe and greater social heights.)

"Close friendships" with some titled names, some figures in the worlds of art and literature, some playboys of distant eras left to the imagination the nature of the relationships. The circumstances surrounding her demise were muddled enough to imply a range of possibilities, some of them wildly implausible. There had been no terrorists in evidence as far as Margaret could recall, nor any truly berserk guests with concealed weapons. It was unlikely that a reporter had actually gathered facts at the scene. No one who had been there would have spoken to the press. Indeed, no one would be likely to admit to being present. There was a photo of Harpennis House looming up like a giant stone monument to the follies of the moneyed social set.

The *Times* had no story, but the next day's edition would certainly carry a lengthy obituary, citing Helene's tireless (some might say tiresome) efforts for charity. Nayland Harpennis had been a distinguished citizen; his widow's death would allow the *Times* to brush off their dead files and recount his exploits in business and philanthropy.

The *Daily News* had a brief item. Mysterious circumstances were cited. Adjuvant Youth was mentioned. They would enjoy seeing their name in print.

On an intuition, Margaret searched through the litter of newsprint on the floor, found Poppy Dill's column, and chuckled. Poor Poppy. Her doubtful journalistic habits had caught up with her, and all those guests so carefully named would be furious to see the list there is black and white for public consumption. Those dancing feet Poppy had so gleefully celebrated in advance had been abruptly stilled when Helene went face first into the sorbet.

Margaret expected to receive a number of phone calls from friends and acquaintances in the course of the day, most of them less curious about the murder than eager to express their relief at having neglected to buy tickets to the Harpennis Ball.

Kasparian was already at the shop when she rang him at eight-thirty. He had heard the news.

"Tsk," he said. "I don't know why I stay in this business. A customer gone overnight and murdered, if I read the papers correctly. Not a good customer, but all the same an old acquaintance."

"I'm sure she wasn't murdered to harm you personally," Margaret said. "It was rather awful. At the time, it didn't penetrate, but . . . this morning. Ugh. Death is awful."

Kasparian was silent for a moment. "Yes," he said. "Yes, it is. Happily, we are usually sheltered from its more violent forms. You have a suspect?"

"Hundreds," Margaret said.

"I suppose you will take the day off to discuss the event with your friends; the death of an insignificant woman whom someone hated enough for one moment of madness to kill her."

"No. I mean, I would like the day off, but wait." Margaret thought hard. "It couldn't have been a moment of madness. People don't carry cyanide around to benefit balls as a matter of course. Someone planned it. Planned to do it. Knew ahead of time that he wanted to kill her. This is dreadful."

"There are those with murder in their hearts," Kasparian said. "I have known them. They are always prepared. And they are not always the sociopaths of the street. It would be convenient for the authorities to contrive to pin it on one of these Youth she gave money to."

"They were there, a few of them," Margaret said. "But it's not their style."

"Correct," Kasparian said. "I merely said convenient, in the sense that the police would then not have to deal with these high-society people, who close ranks when unwanted attention is focused on them. All right, take the day. There won't be much business."

"Kasparian, there were only three hundred people there last night, not a third of them have ever heard of you, and fewer have ever considered buying an expensive bit of jade from you."

"Nevertheless, no one of the world that can afford my prices will be out buying today. You keep me informed."

*One of the bright lights of charity and social grace in our city has been dimmed, has gone out forever.*

Poppy Dill rested back on the mound of pink satin pillows at the head of her bed and reread the sentence. She liked it. She would write a stunning memorial for Helene that would make amends (not that she felt she had to) for writing up the Harpennis Ball about as incorrectly as one could get. The editor at the paper had pointed that out to her in a brief, scathing phone call this morning, although he knew quite well that she didn't like to be wakened too early.

She could imagine the distorted reports that were flashing across the city on red-hot telephone wires or being delivered in person in bedrooms and breakfast rooms along Park Avenue, up and down Fifth Avenue, on the quiet cross streets in the East Sixties and Seventies, along Central Park West. Morley Manton had already called her with a brief, breathless summary. Even at this early state, she could readily imagine dramatic if trivial motives for a number of the attendees and, from personal knowledge or suspicion, really sound reasons for others to do Helene in. But contemplation of that could wait. Now Poppy began to cover page after page of moving words for the afternoon edition. No mention of murder. That would be in poor taste.

Poppy paused to call the newspaper and located one of

the very junior reporters who occasionally did her legwork when her files didn't hold the answers.

"Find out who runs the foundation now, could you?" Poppy said. "Do we know all the trustees? Who might have wanted her dead? Besides that unspeakable Sara de Bouvet, who never has enough money. I could give you copies of Sara's sales receipts from Paris shops that would feed your family for a year. Is there a will? Who benefits? Forget about the son, concentrate on the others. You know the stuff I need."

The reporter was willing. In exchange for such favors, he received half of the flood of free tickets to gala premieres, well-catered cocktail parties, and exclusive gallery openings that poured into Poppy's mailbox.

Poppy went on happily accumulating a list of adjectives with which to memorialize her friend. Some she planned to put in her later piece about Helene's funeral.

"I will attend the funeral," she told herself bravely, "and I shall wear my black Chanel. It's ageless." It was also aged, since it had been devised eons ago by Madame Chanel herself. Poppy never threw anything away.

Robert de Bouvet had not fully recovered by the morning, and Sara had not recovered at all. Both lay abed at the Harpennis apartment on Fifth Avenue. The police had postponed an interview the night before, since both had been prostrated by the evening, but not necessarily by Helene Harpennis's death.

Claire reported to the several acquaintances of Sara's and Robert's who phoned early that they were unavailable for the day. Then she went away to her room to shed more tears at the loss of Madame, of whom she had been quite fond. Between sniffs, Claire thought about how she would proceed with her life now that a handsome salary and other bonuses had been cut off. She could easily find a position

among Madame's friends, but she aspired to being other
than a lady's maid.

Her uncle's formula, which gave Madame such energy
in spite of her age, might have an excellent market. There
were more than enough wealthy old women within a dozen
blocks of the Harpennis apartment alone to give her a se-
cure income if she could establish a business. Madame had
admired Mr. Manton's business sense, although she had
lately been less than kind in her personal opinion of him.
He might be willing to give her assistance, for a modest
share of the proceeds. Claire calculated potential profits,
and that eased her grief. Under no circumstances, however,
did she plan to suggest to police authorities that she might
know anything about anything.


Morley Manton had spoken to the police at Harpennis
House after Helene's murder and had deftly shielded the de
Bouvets from their questions. Then he had seen the grieving son and his wife home, carefully calculating how Robert's goodwill would stand him in good stead in the future.
Morley suspected that the shock Robert was experiencing
had less to do with his mother's death than with the prospect of sudden, great wealth.

As early as he could on Friday morning, he phoned
everyone worth calling:

"A simple case of cold-blooded murder, perpetrated by
that gang of pet bandits Helene kept in funds. You know,
Adjuvant Youth. I warned her a hundred times."

For those who presumed to remind him that but one day
before he had been an enthusiastic sponsor of the Youth, he
said that he was merely repeating the police line. Naturally
he knew exactly who had done it.

Quite a number of people who hadn't planned to attend

Morley's cocktail party on Friday changed their minds and accepted.


As Margaret and millions of New Yorkers read the papers and shook their heads at the follies of the upper classes, or (for the upper classes) the folly and bad luck of being exposed to unpleasantness and scandal, Paul struggled awake and faced the prospect of calling his superior at the bank.

The vice-president-in-charge-of-Paul-Castrocani had someone check on Paul's story. Yes, Paul had attended the ball and had been interviewed by the police. No, there was no suggestion that he was involved in a crime. Nevertheless, the vice president was not quite sure about the Castrocani boy, despite assurances from Benton Hoopes that he was basically all right in spite of an undisciplined upbringing and that Italian blood.

Paul lay in bed a while longer and tried to think how to manage his life. Mrs. Harpennis was a lesson: life was uncertain at best, and deadly at worst. Even for the likes of her, there was no defense. Less so for the likes of Paul.

He remembered a Mafia slaying he had once come upon when visiting Palermo. A man's body in a narrow cobbled street in a pool of blood. An old weeping woman in black, the man's mother perhaps, herself widowed by violence. He had looked for a moment and turned away, gone out of the city into the Sicilian countryside under blue skies in the heat of the sun. No one would ever know whose hand had fired the shots in that secret, closed society. He wished he would never know whose hand had struck down Mrs. Harpennis either, but in the end, he would probably read the name in the newspapers or hear it from one of his dancing acquaintances. It would be someone he knew.

De Vere, he thought, must have seen much worse in his time than the ladylike if troubling demise of Helene Harpennis, but he had remained detached and cool. Paul wished he were so hardened to dealing with the cruelties of life and death.

The sun was well up now, streaming into the nice apartment near Tenth Avenue in the Twenties where he lived. The place belonged to his mother, for no reason anyone had explained except that she had acquired it somehow between his princely father and Benton Hoopes. Carolyn Sue did not easily dispose of possessions once possessed, especially real estate.

"Chelsea's not quite the place, is it, for my kind of life-style," Carolyn Sue had once remarked. "But I must hang on to the place. You never know when some big ol' bank is going to hanker to build a skyscraper right in your backyard barbecue."

She granted the apartment to Paul rent-free, and Benton reminded him periodically that he was fortunate to have that living expense taken care of. The one drawback was that once or twice a year his mother swooped down from the friendly skies into Manhattan and hid out with him instead of staying at the Pierre. This enabled her to shop clandestinely, lest word of her purchases leak back to Dallas and Houston before she had a chance to spring them in person in the right setting.

The duplex had two bedrooms on the second floor, along with a study. Downstairs between the living room and the kitchen was a small bedroom, large enough to be a generous closet, only barely large enough for his mother to refer to it as "the servant's room." Even as Mrs. Harpennis passed from the galas of this world to those of the next, Paul had been contemplating a steady source of income in the form of a paying roommate, who need never know that Paul himself paid no rent. Thousands of young men and women flocked daily to the golden towers of New York and all were in need of a place to live.

He wanted someone who would not be bothered if his

mother did show up; who was reasonably neat, limited his or her intake of controlled substances, and kept hours that did not interfere with his. He had to establish the right connections. Margaret might have practical suggestions.

The phone rang.

"Yes?" A technique for putting on the defensive those he might not wish to speak to.

"Darlin', what are y'all doing up there in New York?"

It was his mother, at her deep Texas best.

"The usual. How are you, Mother?"

"The *usual*? Gunnin' down harmless old ladies? I'm just about the same, thank you for asking."

"You've heard about Mrs. Harpennis already?" The swift spread of news was amazing. It was only nine o'clock in Dallas. "And she wasn't gunned down. She was..." He stopped. "It might have been a heart attack." He would not mention murder.

"Not what I hear," Carolyn said. "And I heard it from two people, as well as the man from that bank of yours. I heard that you were there, dancing with her right when it happened."

"It didn't happen in my arms," Paul said. "I didn't do it. *La vera verità.*"

"Oh, I know that. You're too nice a boy. But I did want to hear the truth from you. If you can't trust your own flesh and blood, who can you trust? Your sweet ol' daddy taught me that."

Paul could never think of the tall, distinguished, magnetic Aldo as a "sweet ol' daddy."

"I don't know much, *principessa*." Why not remind her who dear old dad was? "I think someone must have poisoned her. It was crudely done on the surface, but with three hundred people there, many with the opportunity, maybe it was very subtle."

"I could think of a hundred or so who'd like to see her gone. I used to run into Helene all over the place when I was living in Europe. And didn't she love to be courted by all those counts and lords and such? Not to mention the others. The men who were . . . you know . . . not quite the thing. Good-looking Communists and Albanian sheepherders and waiters, and never mind the consequences. No sense at all about men except when it came to marrying. Then handsome didn't count. Money did. She was no spring chicken, even then, but she did all right for herself. Exactly who was there last night?"

He made a stab at giving her an orderly list.

"Mrs. Harpennis's son and daughter-in-law."

"That tart," Carolyn said. "In principle she's willing and able, if she'd take the time from chasing around with gigolos."

"Basil Jones, Morley Manton, Miss Sheridan, a Mrs. Nagy who was supposed to be a great friend . . ."

"Why, honey, you're just namin' all her *servants*. I want to know who was there who matters."

"Ambassador Duckworth. He remembers you well—almost as clearly as Mrs. Harpennis does. Did. I saw Countess Cloissoné, but I didn't speak to her. I feared she might remember that time I knocked her into the sea at Portofino. Goneril Gmymth was with some Saudi sheik."

Carolyn sniffed. "Purely business, I'm sure. Goneril has always preferred the company of women. It's broken her father's heart. And those Arab fellows . . . well, never mind about them."

"I sat with Charles Stark and his wife at dinner. Dianne."

"Now that's the kind of people I like you to associate with. Dianne's a bright little thing who's worked her way up in society like a real trooper. Not a snob."

"She has a sister."

"There you are. A real nice family, and Charlie's well-off."

"Leila Parkins was there, too."

Carolyn Sue chuckled. "She even makes the Dallas papers, honey. Awfully rich, but wild."

"Even some of the Adjuvant Youth came. The ball was to raise money for whatever they do in some unsavory part of the city. They appeared to be some sort of ethnic gang."

"No! Then Helene died just in time, rest her soul. Trust me, darlin', nobody really wants to be associated with supporting a street gang. That kind of radical chic went out years ago. Her next charity ball would have been filled up with people off bus tours from New Jersey."

Paul loved his mother. Nips and tucks around the eyes and decades of peroxide hadn't damaged her common sense at all.

"I promise I'll tell you anything I find out," Paul said. "Margaret Priam and I might even be meeting with the police."

"Lady Margaret is too old for you."

"We happened to be leaving the ball at the same time, and happened to get involved. Margaret was quite taken with the police detective."

"Ah, those upper-class English girls."

"Give my best to Ben," Paul said. "Tell him I'm starving."

"Oh you . . . You call and tell me all the gossip. And I'll put a little check in the mail. You might have to buy a new suit to testify in court. Don't buy Armani. He's not right for you."

"I doubt I will be called upon to testify," Paul said. "I am merely a person who was on the fringes. Margaret feels the police aren't going to have an easy time sorting it out."

"It will be swept under the Aubusson," Carolyn said. "Paul, honey, these are not honorable people. I don't know but what you ought to get away from that city. It's dangerous."

"I've always liked Paris," Paul said.

But his mother had hung up.

# Chapter 5

"**Y**ou will be surprised," Margaret said, as she filled a Waterford tumbler to the brim with fresh grapefruit juice, "that I retain much of my early training in domestic culinary arts."

"You were married, then? May I ask?"

"You may. I was. Someone from back home in England. Socially unimpeachable, but a chinless wonder, long on family name, short on pounds and pence to make up for the limited horizons. It was a mistake, and it didn't last long. I had a little girl, since you will next ask about children. She died young, and no, don't make sympathetic noises. She was not right all her short life. After a good deal of anguish, I concluded that it was for the best. She would never have been well."

Margaret turned on her heel and disappeared into the compact white kitchen. After a moment, she called out, "Did you see the papers? Poppy Dill mentioned you in her column. You'd have some invitations out of that in any case, and now all the more since you were there last night."

He followed her out to the kitchen. Margaret was skillfully finishing a huge, perfect, fluffy omelet.

"I can use the free meals," Paul said, "but under those

circumstances . . . This killing of Mrs. Harpennis is most peculiar."

"Peculiar. Mmm. I'll tell you what's peculiar. I've been thinking about it. Helene was not a universal favorite, but one doesn't do murder because she let something slip about someone's old love affair, or a family tree that wasn't quite perfect, or any such silly reason. It must have been deadly serious."

"And not a mistake?" Paul took an indicated place at the dining table laid with beautiful antique silver, fragile old Bohemian china, and snowy linen. Three white roses stood in a slim crystal vase at the center.

"Never a mistake," Margaret said. "I told Kasparian that a person doesn't carry poison around on a lark. It's the sort of thing you plan in advance."

"Like the hidden capsule of cyanide to bite on and swallow if captured by an enemy agent?" Paul was not a great reader, but he was fond of spy tales. "None of the diplomats I met last night seemed that type."

"Heavens, I shouldn't think anyone in Helene's set was spying for the enemy, not even poor old Ducky Duckworth, who never was much of a success ambassadoring in all those dreadful little countries they sent him to." Margaret passed Paul the bread, crusty and Italian like the loaves sold in the village near the Castrocani villa, not far from Rome, where Paul had spent his childhood.

"A definite someone set out to kill Helene." Paul didn't like the way that sounded as he said it.

"Right. One could probably eliminate those who saw Helene all the time. Surely they could find a less dramatic and safer venue for doing her in."

"Such friends she had," Paul said. "You saw how they trampled each other to depart at the first hint of trouble."

"And hints are the only thing the police will hear from those so-called friends," Margaret said, "if they hear anything at all. By this time, whoever is in charge must be gnashing his teeth in frustration. I rather doubt that you and I will be interviewed at all." She sounded disappointed.

"I believe that detective liked you," Paul said.

She brushed it aside. "He would think he did, for a time. Briefly. People like that are taken with titles, and so was he, despite his sarcasm. He wasn't really my type, although attractive in a way."

Paul hesitated before he spoke. "Margaret, I do not like the idea of getting involved, although I also do not like the idea of murder. Surely it must have been one of the few who were closest to Helene at the moment of her death."

"You're right," Margaret said. "But I can't think why any one of them would do it. Except Sara, of course, whose moral sense is so ill developed that she might not be aware that murder is wrong. But then, she's American."

Margaret came back from the kitchen with a plate of cheese—a chunk of Gruyère, a crumbly bleu, and some creamy Taleggio, another Italian touch for Paul.

"The point," Margaret said, "the frightening point, is that we know someone—know them by name or sight or family connection—who planned to murder and did the deed. And I can't imagine that sort of person."

"Violent feelings do not exist among the highborn of your country?" Paul asked. "There are certainly examples of violent tendencies among my father's family, dating back to the days of the Sforza cardinal during the Renaissance. Then, too, I feel certain that my Texas grandfather began life as an outlaw."

"Well, my great-grandfather, whom I knew in his last years, went out one day when he was young, in a thundering rage, to shoot a neighbor. Reason unknown. He succeeded in wounding the man. Bad behavior in Edwardian England, and he got shipped off to the Colonies for a time till it was forgotten. He wasn't a cold-blooded murderer, though. It was more like a bit of fictional drama."

"It seems to me that none of what happened last night

took place in an altogether real world," Paul said. "It was more like watching a film. The way poor people live the rich life vicariously, which is something I am getting used to, now that I myself live in poverty."

Margaret raised an eyebrow.

"No really," Paul said. "These stamps for buying food are next, if I can determine the requirements. First I must find a roommate to share the rent."

Margaret chuckled. "We all tread a fine line financially, but surely your own mother doesn't charge you rent."

"How do you know that?"

"How does one know anything? People talk. And your mother is colorful. People especially like to talk about people like her. But don't worry. You don't imagine that any of those people at the ball last night pay for anything they don't have to, do you? Not they. Borrowed jewels, free couture gowns, the company limo . . .I am quite as shameless as they, since I am expected to live up to a certain style without having all that much to do it on. The commissions from Kasparian are useful."

She paused in collecting the plates and looked at her watch. "I guess we are not going to be needed after all by Mr. De Vere's colleague. A pity, too, because I had a hundred calls this morning. I'd like to be able to tell an embellished tale the next time around. Ah."

The phone was ringing. The answering machine played its message for them to hear.

De Vere scarcely spoke two words at the sound of the tone before Margaret picked up the receiver and flicked off the machine. Paul heard her say only, "Yes, yes, yes," before she hung up. When she sat down with him, she wore a pleased smile.

"I hope you can stay awhile," she said. "Detective De Vere has decided it would be best if he came round to interview us again. Something about his superiors persuading him that he was best suited to deal with the likes of us. I can't help feeling, though, that he might have done the persuading."

"I have to admit that I haven't quite gotten a good grasp of this," De Vere said. He sat in the middle of the chintz sofa with his legs stretched out in front of him. He still wore jeans and a windbreaker. Paul observed that his loafers were both expensive and highly polished. He imagined De Vere sitting up in a high chair in one of the city's ubiquitous shoe-repair shops having the dark brown leather buffed to a gloss by a chatty old dark brown man. He did not see De Vere sitting down at the police station with a can of polish and a brush.

Margaret and Paul had moved armchairs side by side to face him.

"What precisely. . .?" Margaret was distracted by the round-faced young man in a sport coat of a distressing shade of green who had been introduced by De Vere as "my partner Bergen." It seemed that the police had no first names.

"What precisely do you not have a good grasp of?" Margaret adjusted the crease on her dark gabardine slacks so it fell exactly over her crossed knee, and leaned forward to indicate deep interest in his answer.

"These people—"

"Ah . . ." Paul was sorry his sigh had been so audible. De Vere now looked at him.

"You have a comment?"

"Me? No." Paul sank back into his chair, but this did not hide him from De Vere's gaze. He seemed to be amused by Paul's discomfiture.

"Please feel free to comment," De Vere said, "whenever the spirit moves you." He took several folded papers from his jacket. Bergen whipped out a notebook and clicked a retractable ballpoint, poised in an everything-you-say-will-be-taken-down-and-used position.

De Vere scanned his papers. "Are either or both of you

acquainted with: an Honorable Dwight Duckworth and Mrs. Duckworth, Count and Countess Cloissoné, Freddy Ravage, Miss Goneril Gmymth—"

"That's pronounced *Smith*," Margaret murmured.

"Ali ben Hassan, Norman Gregg, Halliday Monckton, Mrs. Reeves Benedict..." He appeared not to notice that Margaret and Paul were nodding at every name. "...Charles Stark and Dianne Stark, Peter Pomfrette, the Honorable Cassandra Bley, Gedney Renfrew, Count Erik —something, Eduardo Cruz..."

"Who?" Margaret and Paul spoke as one.

"Never mind," De Vere said. "*I* know him." He folded up his papers and returned them to his pocket. "We've spoken to a number of people who were at the ball. They were not willing to comment. In fact, I have seldom seen so many obviously innocent people eager to retain a lawyer to speak for them. The upshot was they claim to know nothing, have seen nothing, to be only vaguely acquainted with Mrs. Harpennis or any of the others who attended. The same is true of her son and his wife, and those directly involved with the ball—Miss Parlons, Mr. Jones, Mr. Manton, and Miss Sheridan. I find this remarkable, since clearly everyone knows everyone else very well indeed."

"I don't believe," Margaret said vaguely, "that anyone really knows Dr. Emil Glass. He asked me to dance and told me he had always thought a slight overbite was quite delightful, although not dentally ideal."

"Or even Dr. Mittman, by his own admission," Paul said.

"Or the Adjuvant Youth. You see," Margaret said happily, "there are a lot of unknowns."

"Lady Margaret, in your way, you are being as obstructive as the rest. Out of three hundred there, almost everyone knew Mrs. Harpennis."

"And you find this suspicious?" Margaret leaned forward again, chin on hand.

Paul thought she might be overdoing deep concern. Then he noticed that De Vere was watching her with an interest that did not seem to be connected with the ugly corpse that had emptied the ballroom at Harpennis House faster than a rumor that the stock market had plummeted or that Tiffany's was holding a going-out-of-business sale. He also wondered what Bergen could be writing down so busily.

"It's a closed circle, that group," De Vere said finally. "Impenetrable."

"Aha! You think we can help you break in?" Margaret had a dangerous gleam in her eye.

"If you would. You are both at home in this set, you know them. I don't suggest that you do the work of the police, I just want a line on the undercurrents. The gossip."

"For the gossip, I'd suggest you go to someone like Poppy Dill," Margaret said coldly. "She's more or less a clearinghouse for everything that goes on socially—and ever has gone on. I suppose she doesn't print half what she knows."

Bergen was writing it all down furiously. De Vere looked puzzled.

"The lady who writes the social column," Margaret said. De Vere obviously didn't read "Social Scene" and was waiting for further clarification. "You know, the way Eugenia Sheppard used to and Suzy does now. Liz Smith doesn't use a lot of society items in her column. Billy Norwich does, though."

De Vere merely shook his head.

"People like to see their names in print when they contribute to charity or go to one of these parties in the company of other very social people," Margaret explained patiently. "Poppy prints it in her column. Everybody's happy, and Poppy knows simply everything about everyone."

"I'll keep that in mind," De Vere said. "Was she there last night?"

"Hardly." Margaret said. "She's wise enough to stay home."

"I'm afraid hearsay isn't good enough."

Margaret was astonished. "But isn't that what you're asking from me? Asking me what I know or have heard, and then to turn on my own kind—or turn them in?" Before he could answer, she went on, a bit too sweetly. "Perhaps I could be of help in arranging for you to meet these people personally, at some social gathering or other. Cocktails before the theater, or a charity auction. They're quite amusing. Not to worry, Mr. De Vere. I'll fix up something nice for you and Mrs. De Vere."

"That won't be necessary," De Vere said. "There isn't time. Murder is considered urgent business, and a sociological rather than a social affair. In any case, Mrs. De Vere has retired from the business." He went right on without clarifying his marital status. "I need advice. We do rely on informants occasionally. I thought you might oblige . . . out of family feeling. I don't have any clear direction to take in that"—he waved his hand out toward the thin layer of pollution that hovered many stories above the city—"that jungle."

"And the law of the jungle prevails rather than the rule of law?" Margaret said.

"Something like that. I can't say that I care for people who believe they are above the law by virtue of an accident of birth or the accumulation of wealth."

"I can't speak for Paul," Margaret said slowly, "but I will be happy to tell you anything I can. Paul and I had only a distant view of the actual event. And incidentally, I don't think my acquaintances believe they are above the law. At least not most of the time."

"Perhaps not," De Vere said. "But someone put cyanide into a pretty little dessert served up to a well-known and wealthy lady who does many good works for charity. That is an unlawful act. Who might have done that? Why? A friend who was actually an enemy? A person caught up in some dangerous madness? And it was likely someone you know. Doesn't it trouble you?"

"Yes," Margaret said. "Yes, it does." She stood up. "If I think of anything . . ."

De Vere stood and Bergen leapt to his feet. "Let me know," De Vere said. "And . . . Mr.—Prince . . ."

"Paul would be fine," Paul said, and prayed fervently that De Vere would not turn to him as a source of information.

"Paul, I understand you are half-American. Lady Margaret may not feel that she has any responsibility for crime as a guest in this country, a bird of passage so to speak."

"Just a bloody minute," Margaret said. "I pay my taxes."

De Vere raised a hand and silenced her. "But if you have any ideas that might assist us . . ."

"Delighted to help if I can," Paul said desperately. The people at the bank would be appalled. "I doubt that I can be of use."

"We'll find out who did it eventually," De Vere said.

Bergen was already edging toward the door. He had not spoken. Paul wondered if the police in America hired mutes with a highly limited clothes sense on purpose. At a toss of Margaret's head, Paul obediently guided Bergen down the hall. He reached the front door, swung it wide, and looked around behind him. De Vere and Margaret were not to be seen. Then they appeared, strolling down the hall, laughing at something.

"I'm so sorry we couldn't do more for you," Margaret said.

"Understandable, Lady Margaret. If there's anything further, we'll be in touch."

De Vere nodded to both of them graciously. He seemed to be in a good humor. Paul shut the door firmly on Bergen's excruciating coat, greatly relieved that they had escaped the clutches of the law.

"Well!" Margaret sounded jubilant. She took Paul's arm

and led him back to the living room. "Super!"

"I am pleased that we avoided helping De Vere," Paul said. "If people knew I was talking about them to the police, they'd never let me court their daughters."

Margaret threw up her hands and paced the apartment.

"We're not out of anything, love. You and I are going to find out what the police can't. You heard De Vere. Anything we can do to assist."

"I refuse."

Margaret moved the vase of roses an inch to one side, looked at it critically, and moved it back. "You know, I suspect the adorable, rich Leila Parkins would be aroused by the idea that you are helping to corner a criminal, as long as it isn't someone who supplies her with illicit pleasures."

"But you . . . I told him no." Paul weakened.

"Not really," Margaret said slowly. "And he's right in saying that the people who were at the ball are going to obstruct justice if they can. They'll tell big lies to cover up some petty guilts they bear, and they won't mind getting other people in trouble as long as they stay clear. More important, I do not wish to have this person De Vere go through his life thinking that I believe that I and my world — yours, too, come to think of it — are not answerable to the same justice as everyone else."

"I do wish to see justice done," Paul said, "but I refuse to make extraordinary efforts to assist."

"You will," Margaret said serenely. "It will give you a worthwhile occupation. First I am going to harass Sara de Bouvet into revealing all. She and I were briefly schoolgirls together at a horrible school in Switzerland, until she got tossed out because of some incident involving the maths master. I have to have something to tell De Vere tonight . . ."

"Tonight?"

"We have sort of a date this evening. He's divorced, he told me. Isn't that heaven?"

Paul didn't answer. It seemed grossly unfair that a casual cop could attract the attention of a woman like Margaret Priam, while he, in a dinner jacket, with a title, and what some had described as devastating Italian charm, was incapable of dazzling Leila Parkins.

"We'll just help him along a little bit," Margaret said. "Do it for me. And one thing you must do is go to that cocktail party at Morley's tonight. It will be sizzling with gossip."

"Not Morley," Paul protested. "He has the strangest friends."

Margaret pointed to the phone. "His number's in that little red book. By the by, I know almost every eligible rich girl in the city. The Americans, the English, the South Americans. I'm sure you'd like to meet them all, wouldn't you? Intimate gatherings here at my place. The big, big parties—not like Helene's little ball. I get so many invitations, and I'd love to have you escort me. Then there are the carefree weekends in the Hamptons at my friends' houses. And I could fix you up on a cruise or two, no money down . . ."

"*Basta!* Enough!" Paul said. "You are bribing me."

"Naturally. Don't they do that in Italy? It seems a perfectly reasonable method of getting one's way. And it's only Morley. You can take care of yourself."

"All right. I suppose I do want to know who did it, and the only two I know who definitely didn't are you and me. Although," Paul said as he picked up the receiver to dial, "I have great faith in Dr. Mittman's innocence."

The line was busy for three attempts, but when Morley finally answered, he sounded delighted. "Divine people are coming, and they adore princes. Six-thirty until whenever."

"Done," Paul told Margaret. "I am going under protest."

"Listen to everything," she said. "Morley managed to get awfully close to Helene. He was terribly eager not to be thought of as someone in trade, which of course he is."

"He was her friend," Paul said. "They all were."

"Were they? I've been thinking about that. Helene's friends were ambassadors and duchesses and investment bankers. But interior decorators and gofers and glorified secretaries? I wonder."

"My mother did call them her servants."

"Did she?" Margaret looked thoughtful. "Your mother is wise. That is exactly what they are. People to satisfy her needs. Speaking of your mother, I've solved your problem."

"Which one?" His problems were many and monumental.

"A roommate. Paying in cash, and no problems. Straight and mature, employed."

"And that would be?"

"De Vere, of course. He's living in a hotel, can you imagine? And not a real hotel like the Pierre or even the Plaza. A place downtown, full of hookers with rentals by the hour."

"He wants to move to my place?" Paul said.

"He doesn't know it yet, but I'll fix it up."

"Margaret. *Cara mia*, Lady Margaret. No . . ."

"Oh, don't thank me," Margaret said. "What are friends for?"

# Chapter 6

"*Sara darling*. How awful." A mere hour after De Vere's visit, Lady Margaret Priam had changed into a serious brown dress that Paul had recognized as costing at least two weeks of his salary (and admired her greatly for managing it) and swept into the late Helene Harpennis's living room on the butler's heels.

As she brushed cheeks with Sara de Bouvet, Margaret did not miss Sara's venomous look at the butler, but there were not many butlers now in service capable of deflecting Margaret when she was intent on a goal. The Harpennis butler's statement that Madame de Bouvet was not receiving had not in the slightest halted her forward motion.

"It has been trying," Sara said. "Robert is not taking it well." She did not suggest that Margaret sit.

"I should think not," Margaret said. "He was so very close to his mother."

With that statement, which was uttered with recognizable insincerity, Margaret sat anyhow.

"It's good of you to stop by," Sara said, "but I have a frightful headache." She had the appearance of an anorexic black stork huddled under a haystack. In the name of fashion, someone had done something unspeakable to her hair.

She actually did not look at all well, but Margaret put that down to a diet of arugula and valium plus the indulgences of the preceding evening. It surely wasn't prostrating grief.

"I'm only up because the lawyers are due any minute to discuss the funeral. Robert isn't able to deal with it, but can you believe—Basil Jones actually wanted to arrange it all. As though he had rights and privileges in this family."

"Basil, yes. Exactly what is he?" Margaret sounded guileless, but she and Paul had agreed finally—Paul with some reluctance—that it was their duty to press for information that might be purposely obscured for the police. Margaret promised she could annoy Sara enough to make her speak without thinking. It seemed to be working.

"Basil is a pain in the ass," Sara said. "As soon as this is over and done with, so is he, with his stupid airs. The old creep has the nerve to talk to me in French." She flounced to an armchair that seemed to be covered in shiny black silk and threw herself into it. Although Sara had attended and been removed from some of the finest schools for young ladies around the world, no one could claim that she had been educated in any of them.

Margaret composed herself regally in her chair. "You don't care for him then? He was terribly devoted to Aunt Helene."

"Aunt?" Sara's voice rose several octaves. "She was no more your aunt than . . . than I am."

"Heaven forbid, dear. Not technically. She was sort of . . . well, we called it married for a time to that relative of Daddy's. I was only a tiny girl." At the age of five, one always believes that a grown-up man and woman sharing a room must be married. Under present circumstances, Margaret felt no guilt that she might be overstating a relationship she had observed from the nursery. "Besides, she and Mummy were chums. I think they first met during a London season, right before the war. Anyhow, I used to call her aunt."

"What a bloody lie. You were always good at that."

"Nothing but the truth from these lips, Sara darling. I believe he was one of the ones Helene was always leaving Henri de Bouvet for. Those little scandals were long before your time. This one lasted no time at all, over and forgotten before almost anyone had a chance to enjoy it. They secluded themselves at the Priory."

"You're making this up. What Priory?"

"Our family place in England, Priam's Priory. The Tudor bits still hold up in spite of being rather cold and draughty in the winter. Surely you've been there. American tourists love it. Not quite National Trust, but definitely Historic Houses Association. My brother rents it out to film companies. In any event, " Margaret said slyly, "she went back to France and Henri de Bouvet in order to rescue poor young Robert from a life of mucking about in the vineyards. But you'd know more about that. I hear there wasn't much de Bouvet money for Robert in the end."

Sara leaned forward, her ghostly face emerging from the gloom of the black background. "This is preposterous nonsense. Helene had her flings when Robert was little, but she didn't divorce de Bouvet until much later. The divorce killed him, he simply wasted away, and Robert got everything that was left." Sara did not need to confirm aloud that what Robert got was not what Sara had counted on. "Now this mess."

"How fortunate you are to have excellent lawyers about to handle the unpleasant details," Margaret said.

Lawyers seemed a subject to engage Sara's interest and ire.

"Handle." Sara snarled. "They will drive me to distraction with their 'handling.' They beat around the bush, won't tell me a thing I need to know, and charge I don't know what an hour to do it. At least they don't plan to turn this into a state funeral, the way Basil did. I simply want to get it over and get the legal things cleared up."

"Helene deserves a major funeral, surely," Margaret said. "She and the foundation were such a force for good in the city. I don't suppose you know what becomes of the foundation now."

Sara narrowed her eyes. "If you're trying to pump me about Helene's will," she said, "it won't do any good. The details haven't been made known, even to the family. Naturally, one expects . . ."

Sara left her expectations unspoken. But naturally her expectations were grand.

"I presume the foundation will go on forever," she added bitterly. The lawyers will explain about that, then Robert"—Margaret understood that to mean Sara—"Robert will see that Helene's hangers-on take their proper places in the scheme of things."

"Would Robert like to take over for his mother as head of the foundation? Or perhaps you would?"

Sara looked at Margaret as though she had taken leave of her senses. "I certainly don't have time for that sort of thing—meetings and decisions. Naturally, I do have definite ideas about the right way to use the foundation's funds. Helene never understood that there are some quite, quite needy people abroad."

Margaret easily saw that Sara was thinking of quite, quite deprived persons living in France, burdened by taxes and creeping socialism. Robert and Sara de Bouvet, for example. They had their perfectly nice home in the country amidst the vineyards, and a flat in Paris, but nowadays one never did have quite enough francs to cut a proper swath in the Bois. And to climb the social ladder into the salons of the likes of Marie-Helene de Rothschild and Jacqueline de Ribes—it required an excess of cash merely to put one's foot on the first rung.

"We'll dispose of this apartment," Sara said. "I can't imagine why Helene thought she needed all this space. She could as easily have stayed in a corner of Harpennis

House. The third-floor bedrooms are all unused. This place should sell for a couple of million at least."

Sara stood up, the last vestiges of attention dissipated by her hangover. "I'm so glad we could have this little chat, Margaret. But I'm terribly busy."

Margaret didn't move. "Have you spoken with the police?"

"They were about last night," Sara said. "I didn't have anything to tell them. Helene had dreadful acquaintances in the old days, bearded Communists and the like. I know her murder was part of a plot. Anyhow, I was too shocked and grief stricken to speak. The police understood."

Margaret assumed that even the police, and especially De Vere, could recognize a Moët overdose.

"That officious Manton man dealt with them. I've never liked him," Sara said. "He is largely to blame for this, I think." Her arm swept the expensively decorated room, which was not to Margaret's taste but had probably been very much to Helene's. She had always had a firm grasp of what she liked, and that included ostentatiously luxurious surroundings. Porthault linens on the beds, Baccarat crystal on the sideboard, water lilies by Monet on this wall, a nice Cézanne on the other.

Sara wasn't finished. "Manton actually had some idea that Helene might name him a trustee of the foundation to replace that man who died. A decorator, indeed. And I do wish someone would do something about silencing that Mrs. Thing . . . Nagy. She's called three times to speak to poor Robert, as though she deserved consideration. I never could abide her. She was always turning up with Helene, putting it about that she was so close to her and Robert. I instructed the butler to tell her when the funeral was, but even that wasn't enough. She claims Helene had promised a show of paintings for some dead husband. I won't have her or any of them here in my house."

Sara had easily made the transition from being a visitor

in her mother-in-law's apartment to the lady of the house.

Her wrath was not yet exhausted. "And would you believe that Helene's maid refused to lift a finger for me. I tell you, no servant of mine would dare to behave that way. I wanted to get her out of the house at once, but Robert insists that she stay until after the funeral, since she's been with Helene forever."

"Tsk," Margaret said, brightening at the mention of a loyal maid. "Servants are a trial. Helene's maid?"

"Claire. A Swiss," Sara said. "I've never trusted the Swiss. Too clever by far."

"Ah, yes," Margaret murmured. "You have the same happy memories of our school days in Switzerland as I do."

"Weren't you dismissed for some offense?" Sara was growing restless and was likely to turn really mean. She was eyeing a table at the end of the room where a row of crystal decanters promised soothing relief from the difficulties of this visit to New York.

"Surely that was you, darling," Margaret said. "I was never offensive in my life. Mummy wouldn't allow it. She instilled in us principles of clean living and respect for authority. I suppose you do have information for the police?"

"What? No. I was standing about nearby with Robert but I hardly saw a thing. When Helene started tearing into those people who do things for her, I wasn't interested in hearing, but then Morley came running out of the library to find out what was happening—naturally he stopped to make improper suggestions to one of those fey little waiters. Vicious man. I wouldn't be surprised if he knocked Helene off."

"I suppose you'll tell the police all this?"

"Heavens no. Why should I do their job for them? I made it very clear that others were handling the details of the murder."

"Very wise," Margaret said, and swept out even as she had swept in. Over her shoulder she saw Sara heading toward the decanters.

The butler met Margaret at the door. Margaret did not live in fear of servants: the fear that they would quit, the fear that they would reveal desperate secrets, or that they or their confederates might steal judiciously the tiny jewels, the bits of cash, the small piece of valuable porcelain or silver among the many. She had grown up with faithful family retainers, people who had worked on the estate for all their lives. It was different if one surrounded oneself with servants later in life, along with newly acquired riches and social position.

"I'm so sorry about Mrs. Harpennis," she said. "You must feel the loss personally."

"She was very kind," the butler said. "A very generous lady." Something in his tone indicated that he felt Madame de Bouvet, on the other hand, was neither kind nor generous, and he did not at all regret allowing Margaret in to see her.

"I understand Claire was devoted to Mrs. Harpennis. Please convey my condolences."

"I will do that, Lady Margaret."

"And, yes . . ." Margaret appeared to have a sudden bright thought. "I know Claire must feel greatly at sea now, since she is not a native in this country. You might also tell her that I will ring her, since I may have a suitable place for her with a very distinguished lady here in the city."

"I am sure Claire will be grateful for your interest, Lady Margaret."

Margaret's interest lay only in finding out if Claire could be persuaded to let fall information that might shed light on the mystery of Helene Harpennis's death. Servants were privy to secrets that one's dearest friends and closest relatives were not. If anyone could persuade her to give up old secrets, it was Lady Margaret Priam.

Margaret emerged onto the street. The sun was starting to sink behind the buildings on Central Park West, far across the Park. She wondered how Paul was getting on. By dint of further bribes, she had persuaded him to visit Nina Parlons at Harpennis House while she was seeing Sara.

"Nina's a darling girl, and terribly clever," Margaret had assured him. "She's not at all attached to the foundation, and will give you an objective view."

"She'd do that for the police," Paul had said.

"Ah, but De Vere is merely De Vere, and you are a prince."

Paul had gone.

The sidewalk across Fifth Avenue from Helene's building was crowded with strollers headed home with their children and dogs and significant others. The greatest impact the death of Helene Harpennis would have on most of them would be the continuing and sensational press coverage. They would be treated to the details of her life and estimates of her dollars and would soon enough forget it all, even if someone in her elevated circle were eventually accused of the crime.

True, it was a more diverting murder than the many that occurred daily in the city. Few were deeply stirred by violent acts perpetrated in rubbish-filled alleys behind abandoned buildings in the Bronx or on dark Brooklyn streets, punishment for some deviation from the codes of organized crime, or drug-inspired retaliation, or passion betrayed, or simple robbery gone wrong. Not, in the end, so very different from the emotion that probably caused Helene's death, except that when you color a murder with the green of wealth, the sparkle of diamonds, and celebrity names, and offer a glimpse of the world where society reigns, the masses are fascinated. For a time.

The limousine that pulled up in front of Helene's building was very long and had smoked windows. Since this part of Manhattan was chockablock with limos, few paid them any attention. Normally Margaret would have crossed over to the Central Park side of Fifth without a second glance, but then she saw a pack of men in sober three-piece suits lugging huge briefcases spring from the limo and dash into the lobby of Helene's building. The lawyers had arrived. They would make Sara's day complete.

Margaret crossed Fifth and slowly walked south along the broad sidewalk.

If she turned her back on the clean, solid, canopied apartment buildings that faced Central Park along Fifth Avenue, if she blocked out the sight of the skyscrapers downtown and shut her ears to the traffic, if she looked into the dense trees of the park, could she pretend she was back home in England? Were there peaceful crescents and mews and squares anywhere here in Manhattan to remind her of London? It was a thought that came to her more often lately.

Should she go home and forget about the murder of a basically selfish old woman? De Vere and his colleagues would solve or not solve the crime. Paul was right. It was nothing to do with them.

Yet there was something about De Vere that she liked. And something about the murder that challenged her.

She could always go home to England.

# Chapter 7

*While Margaret* burst upon the unwelcoming Sara, Paul found himself in front of Harpennis House. He was not totally convinced that it was his duty to extract information from Nina Parlons, but Margaret was not to be denied.

Paul had come to Harpennis House armed with a plan of his own devising.

The pale yellowish stone the robber baron had selected for his mansion's outer walls looked anemic, almost hopeless, in the fall afternoon's sunlight. It was a big house, and it was neither warm nor welcoming. In this it reflected perfectly the character of its builder, whose descendants, Paul understood, still enjoyed the fruits of his ill-gotten wealth and were actually proud of their name. It was a building for viewing at nighttime, unlike the geranium and gold and ecru palaces of Rome, which sprang to life in the daylight.

The tall glass doors were covered with an elaborate black iron scrollwork to keep out marauders, and they were firmly locked. Paul pushed the bell and waited. He waited long and patiently, thinking wistfully of his father, Prince Aldo, watching the sunset over the spot where Rome would be if there were no smog, while cheerful *contadini* revved up their motor scooters for a night of jollity and pillage in the countryside. He hadn't seen his father for a couple of years. He wondered if he might get some time off from the bank to recover from the emotional stress of witnessing a murder and catch a cheap flight to Rome. Terrorists, kidnappers, and the hazards of driving in the Eternal City were minimally dangerous compared with Margaret's determination to involve him in a murder and to house a police detective in his apartment.

Paul peered through the grillwork of the Harpennis House doors and thought he saw a face look quickly around a corner at the far end of the interior hallway. He rang again and heard the mellow "dong" echo through the first floor. After another long while, a short, willowy person of indeterminate sex moved tentatively toward the door, hand at brow. Paul gestured encouragingly. Finally the person—it turned out to be an emaciated young man who was possibly wearing makeup—turned a bolt and opened the door a sliver.

"We're closed," he said. "No comment if you're the press, and if you're looking for art, the gallery won't be having a show for two weeks. Watercolors by Ethyl Birch. Sorry."

Paul thought to put his foot in the door, but the entire assemblage of glass, wood, and metal looked to weigh half a ton.

"Wait. I am a friend of Signorina Parlons." The youth fell for the accent immediately and Paul's dazzling smile. "I am Prince Paul Castrocani. Is she in?"

"Oooh. She might be. I'll check."

It was a matter of seconds between the time the youth scampered down the hall and the time Nina returned.

"Paul, sorry you had to wait. We've had all these reporters. I can't imagine why they find this tragedy so interesting. No, I guess I can, but they don't have to live with it, and we do."

Paul followed her down the hall, past the empty white-walled gallery where Helene would no longer be hostess at opening-day receptions for her pet artists. Nina showed him into a small, dark office. There was a chair for him and one for her behind the cluttered desk. She sat, not relaxed. Indeed, with her hair pulled back and dark shadows under her eyes, she looked fragile, as though she hadn't slept for days. "It's not comfortable," she said apologetically. "The regular staff and Mrs. Harpennis have—had—the luxury offices. What can I do for you?"

He leaned forward and turned on every bit of charm he had inherited from his father. "You could accompany me to Morley Manton's cocktail party this evening, if you are not too worn by events."

"Oh, well, I'm managing, and I'm flattered. Under normal circumstances, I'd be delighted, but . . ." She looked at him quizzically, as though she were sorting out his motives for asking. "But there's so much happening here, and there's no one to deal with it. Janine has retreated. She's been shut up in her office all day on the phone. Or else she's burning the evidence. Or planting it." She sounded bitter.

"You don't care for her?"

"She doesn't care for me," Nina said. "She resented me from the day I came to work on the ball. It was just a temporary job for me, a good one, but the foundation is her life. Who could have known? Before Mr. Harpennis died, Janine ran everything, but Mrs. Harpennis had been easing her out. Now she's getting even by not having a thing to do with the murder. I thought I could count on Basil Jones, but he's vanished. Before the ball he was around day and night. At least the foundation lawyers are dealing with the funeral arrangements. I'm trying to handle things at this

end with Max, the boy who let you in. He works here
part-time, but he's a bit . . . flighty."

"But why did you not ask me to assist you?"

Nina laughed. "What a thought!" Paul was taken aback
by her amusement. He thought of himself as a reasonably
capable man in a crisis. Once he'd even rescued a very
voluptuous young woman from drowning off the beach at
Saint-Tropez while the rest of the suntanned troops stood
about flapping their hands.

"Oh, don't look hurt," Nina said. "I meant it's mostly
phone calls that I can put off or refer. It's usually been the
press, or friends of Helene's from all over the world
who've somehow heard already. I can't imagine how."

Remembering his mother's early morning call, Paul
knew there was a communications network out there that
the phone company might envy. Perhaps the very affluent
used microwave transmissions or had personally owned
satellites.

"You haven't answered me about tonight," he said. "I
came all this way to invite you."

"Really?" He saw she didn't believe him. "Did you
need to come in person to ask? There is a phone."

"Unfortunately, the line has been engaged."

Nina pushed a stray strand of hair out of her eyes and
sighed. "You're right. It has. I guess an escape from all
this would do me good. Yes, I'd like to go with you—as
long as Morley Manton doesn't ask me silly questions. I
don't know if he's a friend of yours, but I don't think he's a
terribly nice person. I blame him for the Adjuvant Youth.
He was the one who talked Mrs. Harpennis into getting
involved with them in the first place and then inviting them
to the ball. They weren't really that awful, though, were
they? Sort of sweet. Oh, yes. I leave with the person I
came with. I don't care for being abandoned by my
escort."

"You think that I have no principles?" Paul was a touch

offended, though he suspected that she was half teasing him.

"It's not that. My work for these charity groups has made me wary of the natives, and that includes you. I prefer to work for big, crass banks that want a really good party and spend a lot of money to get one. The foundation —Mrs. Harpennis—were nice enough, but what with the murder and Janine Sheridan out to get me . . ." She was troubled, and Paul took the opportunity to put his hand on hers. "The idea of murder is so awful."

"Yes, and then there are the police to deal with," Paul said casually. "I suppose they have spoken with you."

"Last night, right after you and Lady Margaret left. That nice Mr. De Vere, and then there were some more here this morning first thing. They went all over the ballroom and the library again. We couldn't let the caterer start cleaning up until this afternoon. He was furious. His people still have to come take away the tables and chairs. Then the police kept after him about his waiters, and who had served the sorbet to Mrs. Harpennis, and who had asked for it. I didn't notice who handed it to her because Mrs. Harpennis was carrying on about Adjuvant Youth getting out of hand. Mrs. Harpennis was upset about several things last night."

"Do you remember anything about how it might have happened? Someone must have noticed someone dropping cyanide into her sorbet."

"I certainly would have told the police if I had," she said sharply. She removed her hand from under his where she had willingly let it lie. "I'm quite an upright citizen, although I can't be certain about the rest of them. They seem so harmless, bent on their little intrigues and gossiping and partying. Basil and Janine. Even Morley. That nice little Mrs. Nagy. Of course, I wouldn't put anything past the de Bouvets. They are both disagreeable." Nina eyed him with suspicion. "Are you trying to find out something from me?"

"Of course," Paul said with a disarming, charming grin. "Who did it."

"It wasn't me," Nina said wearily. Paul thought she looked really very attractive, in spite of being pale and tired. "There were times in the course of the preparations that I would gladly have seen Mrs. Harpennis made silent or unconscious, but never dead." She sighed. "This isn't going to do any good for my reputation as a party planner."

"Nonsense," Paul said. "This will make your star shine all the more brightly. A reputation for creating the sensational benefit. I myself am merely nosy. I can't imagine how such a thing could occur so publicly and no one notice how."

"There is one thing," Nina said slowly. "I didn't say anything to the police, it seemed so silly. It's probably not important, but it wasn't a waiter's arm."

"Excuse me?"

"Mrs. Harpennis was waving her hands and asking for the sorbet. I was trying to slip away. When it arrived, it was handed across all the people around to her. There was an arm, wearing black and a . . . a cuff link, perhaps. Some kind of jewelry. I remember seeing a beautiful round deep turquoise stone with tiny diamonds set in gold. Definitely not waiter's wear. But I didn't see whom it belonged to. Too many people."

"And you told no one?" Paul tried to remember whether he had noticed such cuff links. He couldn't. He hoped Margaret had.

"What could I have told? And I might be wrong. I'd hate to get anyone in trouble because of something I'd half seen. I'd had a couple of glasses of champagne by that time, like everyone else. Who notices everything perfectly under those circumstances?"

Nina shifted nervously. "It can't be important. I don't think it belonged to anyone handing her poison. Well, I still have an awful lot to do. I suppose I'll have to stick around until after the funeral to answer calls, if Janine continues to remain uninvolved. You know what they say about her and old Mr. Harpennis."

Paul tried to look knowing and failed, because Nina laughed and looked guilty. "I really hate gossip, but Mrs. Nagy once told me Janine was always madly in love with Mr. Harpennis. She worked for the foundation long before Helene came along and married him. I think that was about twenty years ago, but Janine stuck with the foundation in case they got divorced so then he could marry her. Good Lord, you don't think Janine murdered Mrs. Harpennis from a sort of delayed reaction to losing Mr. Harpennis?"

Paul did not know anything of the late Mr. Harpennis, except that he was very rich, but he thought it unlikely that Janine Sheridan was ever an object of his passion. On the other hand, he knew of situations in which the lady in question had suffered from maddened delusions that the man would see the light and come around romantically. A certain Carla Brandolini had pursued his own father, he recalled, with frightening single-mindedness.

"Maybe you should speak to Janine," Nina said.

"Me?" Paul was alarmed. "Why would I want to do that?"

"You said you were trying to find out who did it. Well, Janine is right across the hall. And I'm not sure but what she'd be glad to accuse me of almost anything. Ask her."

"Thank you, no. I think I'll leave you to your work, unless there's some way I can assist. And if you remember something else about last night . . ."

"I certainly hope I don't," Nina said. "A murder at a party I've organized is bad enough, but to be the one who comes up with the evidence . . . I'd have to move— to—" She sighed. "No place would be far enough."

"Don't worry," Paul said soothingly. "Shall I pick you up here or elsewhere?"

"My place," Nina said. "West Twelfth Street, just off Fifth, if it's not too much trouble."

"Seven o'clock then? I look forward very much."

Nina smiled. "Me too. I'm almost ashamed to say that it's really very nice of you to ask me."

"Not shameful at all," Paul said. "I like you."

Max hovered outside Nina's office.

"Practically everyone wanted to kill Mrs. Harpennis at one time or another," Max said confidentially, "but she was sweet enough. She only had it in for a few people." He glanced meaningfully at Janine Sheridan's closed office door. "Mrs. H. could be a real terror at times. But you wouldn't actually *kill* her."

"I know," Paul said. If Margaret were here, she would force him to speak to Janine. He sighed. "Would Miss Sheridan be free?"

"She slipped out while you were talking to Nina," Max said. "I happened to be halfway up the staircase and looked over the banister, so she didn't see me. Went into Mrs. H.'s office for a minute and ran off just before you came out. Guilty conscience if you ask me. Isn't this fabulous fun?"

Paul looked down his half-Roman nose at Max. It was a formidable gaze descended from one that had halted the barbarians poised to sack Rome some millennia ago. Max cowered.

"I mean, the publicity and all," Max said weakly, and unbolted the front door. "You know. Have a nice day."

# Chapter 8

*W*hen *Janine* first heard the echoing doorbell ring twice, she was convinced that more reporters were at the door, eager to feed on the tragedy that had befallen the foundation. But she did not move from her desk, as once she might have, to send them about their business. Since last night, everything had changed.

In the years she had been executive director of the foundation, practically from the day Nayland had established it, and long before Helene had entrapped him, nothing like this had happened to sully its great name.

"Discretion and efficiency, my girl," Nayland used to say, "that's what I like." Thanks to her, no news of foundation affairs reached the public, except when she allowed it. What was happening now would have been unthinkable in the old days.

Janine was afraid now. She would be held responsible for this betrayal of the principles of the wonderful man who had left his foundation to a selfish and meanspirited woman with no idea how to use the money and prestige wisely. The very thought of Adjuvant Youth made Janine shudder. She had not been strong enough to keep Helene from driving the foundation headlong to destruction. She had tried to halt the erosion by the little ways at her disposal. She had done what she could to accumulate proof for the trustees as to the kind of person Helene was. Scandalous, greedy, and uncaring. Poor Nayland in his infatuation had never seen that side of her.

Across the hall, the little office Helene kept for herself had yielded up its secrets bit by bit over the past few years, thanks to duplicate keys Janine kept, as the executive director should. She had made copies of old documents and letters and left the originals in place, but since last night, she knew she must enter the office again and remove them. If she did not, the police or Robert or Sara might learn the old, startling secrets they held and take away her one remaining bit of leverage.

Janine heard voices bouncing off the marble walls of the hallway. This was too much. A knot of rage pushed aside her fears and grew. How dare the Parlons girl allow anyone into this house? It was bad enough that Helene had seen fit to supplant Janine in planning the ball, the most important event in the foundation's year. A professional party planner indeed!

She sprang from her chair and opened her office door cautiously in time to see Nina usher Paul into her little cubbyhole. She shut the door quickly before they noticed her. She recognized Paul, one of Helene's new little pets with a flimsy title and facile good looks. Too bad for him. Helene was gone.

Her fear returned, and with it the confusion she had lived with since the night before. She would not speak to the police again about last night. They were as bad as the press in telling the public matters they had no right to know. That Mr. De Vere had looked into her eyes and smiled knowingly, as though he suspected she had wanted Helene dead and gone.

And, of course, she had. She knew there were others who felt the same way.

She placed her fifth or sixth call to Basil, and still he wasn't home. She hung up at the sound of the answering machine with his precise little message about leaving a name and number. She had hours ago left a message to greet him when he returned to his old, high-ceilinged apartment across the city.

Between them, they had taken care of what Nayland had left behind: she had minded the foundation and Basil had served Helene, fetching and carrying and escorting her about to dinners and plays and parties. Janine was at her post, but now, when he was needed most, Basil was missing. Of course Helene's death would change his life as much as it would change hers. But perhaps those changes would have been even greater if Helene had lived to carry out the plans she had hinted at during the ball.

Janine took out the keys to Helene's office and steeled herself to slip in and out as swiftly as possible. It must be done for the sake of the foundation. She opened her door again an inch and listened. She could hear Nina and Paul. A glance down the hall. Max lounged at the doorway to the gallery and eyed her curiously. Disgusting little pervert, hired by Helene naturally. She quickly shut the door, and her heart beat faster.

Had Max been told to watch her while Nina and Paul devised some plan they didn't want her to interrupt? Nina couldn't know or care about anything beyond the ball, but still . . . Nina had been at Helene's table last night as though she belonged there. That prince had appeared with Lady Margaret Priam after Helene had collapsed. She remembered speaking to them at the head of the stairs, but she couldn't remember their questions.

Now Paul was back, asking Nina questions.

The phone on her desk rang and she leapt to answer it. If it was not Basil, then at least let it be Robert de Bouvet. She had left a message for him at Helene's apartment that she must speak with him. If she had any chance to remain with the foundation, it was imperative that she consolidate her postion by reminding him of her loyalty and ability to continue the foundation's work without burdening him.

"Janine?" Belle Nagy's thin voice came as a surprise. "I know it's not the time to trouble you, but I had left some color transparencies of Istvan's important paintings with Helene last night—she put them in the office. She was planning a major exhibit."

"I hadn't heard that, Belle," Janine said. "And I haven't seen any slides about. They may be locked up in Helene's office with the rest of her papers." Then she thought quickly. Belle Nagy might well be of use in fortifying her position at the foundation. "Naturally, I shall have to review Helene's private papers. As an old friend, you understand that many refer to matters one would not like made public. Robert will want me to do it before the funeral, to save him the grief . . ."

"The funeral is Monday according to Helene's butler," Belle said. "You'd have thought Robert would have told me himself."

"It's a difficult time for him," Janine said, "what with the police about, and the lawyers."

"The police," Belle said. "Will they find out who did it? She had enemies, you know. She made enemies. I wouldn't say anything, but someone else might."

"Listen, Belle." Janine said. "I have the press here, and I'm trying to get correspondence cleared up. Nina Parlons is absolutely no help at all. Why don't we have a nice talk after the funeral? I think we can help each other."

"I understand," Belle said. "Thank you."

Janine shook her head as she hung up. The silly woman never understood that Helene had always used her cruelly, without feeling a shred of guilt.

The phone rang again. It was Basil, at last, calling from a pay phone at the Plaza Hotel. She listened while Basil gabbled.

"I understand perfectly how painful it would be for you to return here, Basil, but please try to be calm. I must see you. There are so many things we have to discuss about last night. There are matters that only I know. Our future is at stake."

She listened again. With so many crucial matters at hand, Basil was worried about the account book he used in billing the foundation for his expenses in decorating the ball, and the manuscript of some article on Renaissance medals he was working on for a minor art magazine. He had a deadline, he couldn't face Harpennis House. They were in a large manila envelope in his desk. He had to have them.

"Listen, Basil. I will try to get the things to you." She thought for a moment. "And you must also take some papers of mine and keep them safe. They are personal. I don't want them left in the office. Now?" She looked at her watch. "There are people here. I might not be able to get away." Then she slowly said, "All right. In ten minutes."

The fear edged into her consciousness again. She walked over to the delicate little desk—more of a table with a couple of drawers—where Basil kept a few papers and accounts while working on Helene's projects. There was a manila envelope in one of the drawers, as he had said. It was tightly sealed. She unlocked a drawer of her own desk and took out another envelope. She hoped she could trust Basil to keep it absolutely safe.

She put on her sensible belted beige coat, suitable for fair weather or rain in these autumn days, and peered out her door. Max had disappeared. As casually as she could, she walked to the door of Helene's office and put the key to the lock.

It opened quietly and Janine slipped inside. She knew where to look, and in a second she had stuffed a handful of yellowing papers and letters written in faded ink into her envelope. Then, carelessly tossed into the drawer, she found a handful of color transparencies and some invoices relating to the Youth that Helene hadn't approved before she died. Janine shoved everything into her envelope and felt relief that it was all now safely in her hands. Outside the door again she paused. She heard Nina behind the door of her office saying quite clearly, "My place. West Twelfth Street."

Janine's fear overcame her, and she bolted down the hall and into the empty gallery. Ethyl Birch's watercolors lay stacked in cartons, ready for hanging. Then through the gallery to the little door that led into a back hallway and down the stairs to the old kitchen that seventy-five years ago had served the mansion, before being replaced by modern facilities installed by Nayland on the floor above. Tables and chairs were stacked up ready to be removed that evening by the caterer's men. She darted into the alley behind Harpennis House, where bulging green plastic trash bags held all that remained of the Ball for Adjuvant Youth.

At the top of the little flight of steps onto the sidewalk, Janine paused. Far down at the end of the street, past Madison and Fifth, she could see the trees of Central Park, one or two of them already turning to fall colors.

At the corner of Fifth, as she was about to cross, she saw Lady Margaret Priam strolling carelessly along beside the park wall. The two of them, Margaret and Paul, seemed to be haunting her since last night. She definitely didn't want to have Margaret see her meeting Basil. Then she saw Margaret pause and lean on the wall to contemplate the last green leaves of summer or the debris of the afternoon left on the lawns by park visitors with their hordes of children at play. Janine waited, scanning the sidewalk for Basil.

Two lights changed, and still Margaret did not move, nor did Janine. Then, far down the street, she saw Basil on foot, hunched over and looking furtively at passersby. Janine clutched the two envelopes to her chest and made a decision. Margaret would not see them together.

Margaret had lived long enough in New York not to be surprised to see in the midst of millions a known face. On the opposite side of Fifth, waiting for the light to change, she saw Janine Sheridan hugging two manila envelopes to her chest and searching the walkers on the opposite side of the street. Margaret hesitated and quickly leaned again on the rough stone wall bordering the park. She pondered the value of speaking to Janine here on the street. As she waited and decided, out of the corner of her eye she saw Janine allow two lights to change and still did not cross to Margaret's side of the street. She has seen me, Margaret decided, and she doesn't want to speak to me. Or she hasn't seen someone else and doesn't want to wait.

When Janine suddenly turned on her heel and retraced her steps along the cross street, back toward Madison and then Park where Harpennis House stood on the corner, Margaret surrendered to suspicion.

A surge of traffic led by a parade of city buses and a fleet of cabs prevented her from crossing Fifth against the light. But glancing down Fifth, she recognized Basil Jones flagging a cab. When it angled to the curb, he disappeared in the backseat.

When Margaret finally reached the other side, Janine was far in the distance, almost sprinting back to the solid stone safety of Harpennis House. Margaret had barely reached the east side of Madison Avenue in pursuit when Janine disappeared. Margaret knew she could not have reached Park Avenue and entered Harpennis House by the front door, yet she was gone.

Margaret walked slowly toward Harpennis House, pretending to look at the atrociously expensive items displayed in the boutique windows and examining the subdued brass plates announcing the offices of specialists in dermatology, internal medicine, and nervous diseases. Janine was not lurking in any recessed doorway. When

Margaret reached what was the rear corner of Harpennis House, which almost backed up on a sturdy gray stone building of fairly recent vintage, she discovered a low wrought-iron gate intended to protect the unwary from tumbling down a short flight of cement steps into a narrow alley behind Harpennis House. Janine had evidently slipped through the gate, into the alley, and back into Harpennis House by a servants' entrance.

Curious behavior all around, Margaret thought. Janine Sheridan barely knew her, so her purposeful avoidance of her was queer. Basil on Fifth Avenue could not have been a coincidence.

Harpennis House loomed up, pale and silent, harboring its secrets.

Margaret thought hard for a few seconds to see if there was a loose end that might begin the unraveling. Janine carried two envelopes. Something to give to Basil. She had been forced to return to Harpennis House, envelopes still in hand. For the moment, then, they were in the mansion. Margaret hurried across Park to the southeast corner, where she could observe both the front door of Harpennis House and the sidewalk beside the back alley, and waited.


Janine was breathing heavily when she locked herself into her office, even though the mansion was totally silent and it was clear that the prince and Nina and Max had all departed.

The two brown envelopes lay on her desk. Janine hesitated. Surely it was her duty to see what Basil's envelope contained. For the good of the foundation. With practiced skill she unsealed the end. Papers yes, the account book, and at the bottom, one of Basil's heavy gold rings, handsomely worked into some sort of grotesque figure. She recognized the ring, an antique he claimed had once been the property of some famous old family. She tried to recall when she had last seen him wearing it. She closed her eyes and saw again the Harpennis Ball in a swirl of waltzing colors and Basil's plump fingers bedecked with gold as he bowed to kiss the hand of Mrs. Dwight Duckworth.

Thoughtfully she sealed up his envelope and carried both into the silent hallways of Harpennis House.

At the top of the staircase, she surveyed the dim ballroom. A few stacked tables and chairs remained in the shadows, and pale light from the waning day gave the ballroom a ghostly glow. She crossed the ballroom quickly and entered the little library with its elegant leather sofas and walls lined with bookcases filled with leather-bound volumes from floor to ceiling. She slipped the envelopes behind the row of Balzac novels bound in red leather placed high up on the shelf, and hastily went downstairs.

She dialed Basil's number again, and this time she did leave a message. His envelope was safe, for the moment.


Margaret saw Janine Sheridan leave Harpennis House by the front door. She locked it carefully and slipped the keys into a compact, sensible shoulder bag, too small to hold the envelopes. Then, head down, she hurried south on Park Avenue.

The next step, Margaret decided, was to find Basil, who might be anywhere. She had no idea where he lived, but someone else would.

Margaret caught a cab uptown.

# Chapter 9

"*At last!*" At the sound of her doorbell, Poppy threw off a fluffy mohair blanket and threw on a remarkable shawl that a Spanish duchess had given her in exchange for silence about a tiny scandal in Barcelona.

Margaret stood on Poppy's threshold.

"Lady Margaret, of all people! How delightful."

"I didn't ring ahead," Margaret said apologetically, "and your doorman appeared to be in a stupor from which I couldn't rouse him."

"Those boys," Poppy said as she led Margaret across the marble foyer trailing diaphanous robes. "I believe they tipple a bit in the afternoons. This is a treat. I suppose you're here about Helene. I could have predicted that she'd come to an unfortunate end, but this is more horrible than even I dreamed of. Do sit down."

Poppy sank upon her pillows and Margaret took the deluxe satin chair that Poppy called her "interview" chair.

"I want to hear everything," Poppy said. "I know I can trust you for a clear picture. Basil phoned, but I couldn't make any sense of what he said."

"I know very little," Margaret said, and told her about the ball. Poppy pursed her lips and shook her head.

"Curious. I must know who did it."

She spoke with an odd emphasis so that Margaret couldn't tell whether she meant she was certainly acquainted with the person, or that she would not rest until she knew the murderer's identity.

"Actually," Margaret said, "I was wondering if you could help me."

Poppy looked wary. Sharing was not one of her strong points.

"I need very much to get in touch with Basil. I have no idea where he lives and there are too too many B. Joneses in the phone directory. It has to do with—" Margaret improvised quickly. "I understand that Basil acted as Helene's adviser on art. There was supposed to be a show of Istvan Nagy's paintings that Helene promised to Belle Nagy. Belle asked me to find out what would happen now. I wouldn't want to trouble Robert."

"It seems unlikely," Poppy said. "The show, I mean. Even centuries ago when Helene and Istvan were . . . well, you know . . . she thought he was a fraud as an artist. I suppose Belle Nagy felt Helene owed her something, and even Helene might want have wanted to make amends for old sins." Poppy looked into a distant past. "There were plenty, but only one or two were really damaging to others. Yes, Basil might be aware of something about a Nagy exhibit, but the poor dear is in such a state. You knew, I suppose, that he was confident of . . . um . . . high estate." When Margaret neither admitted knowledge nor questioned her statement, Poppy continued. "I know for a fact that he expected Helene to name him a trustee of the foundation. A desperate desire, it was. Helene wouldn't dream of it, or of . . ." Poppy looked sly. "There were other rumors, but we all know Helene had come to the end of her marrying days."

Margaret was taken aback. "Marriage? Helene and Basil?"

"Purely a fantasy of Basil's," Poppy said firmly. "She was a good thirty years older. But it would have made a delicious story: Helene being married for money instead of the other way around. Anyhow, she could afford to find some sweet young thing, no matter how much she relied on Basil. Someone like that pretty little Prince Paul. Hadn't she quite taken him up?"

Margaret doubted that Paul, even with his claims of direst poverty, would ever have succumbed to the lure of Helene's millions. Aloud she said, "Paul's interest is otherwise engaged."

Poppy looked at her eagerly. Since Paul's infatuation with the idea of Leila Parkins's family assets could scarcely count as a hot romantic rumor, Margaret tried to convey that no hint of what she might know would be allowed to pass her lips. Poppy sighed and picked up a thick, battered leather address book and leafed through it.

"Here's Basil's address and phone number. Lucky man to have managed to hang on to that big old rent-controlled apartment all these years." She wrote out the information.

"Thanks awfully much," Margaret said. "I don't think I'll bother him just now." She spoke with the full intention of bothering him immediately. She stood up. "By the way, about Janine Sheridan . . ."

Poppy dismissed the whole idea of Janine Sheridan with a wide, fluttering gesture. "No love lost between her and Helene. I've never trusted her, to tell the truth. Too secretive for my taste. Fancied Nayland, you know." Poppy eyed Margaret suspiciously. "You aren't trying to find out who did it, are you?"

"Curious is all," Margaret said. "Isn't everyone? Who might have done it, and why, and how."

"Oh, yes," Poppy breathed. "Of course, I have strong suspicions, but absolutely no proof, except that I am capable of putting two and two and another two together to come up with a likely perpetrator or two. You must promise to tell me anything you discover. You know how we journalists are when there's a story to be uncovered. How I'd enjoy having a front-page story."

"You'll be the first to know anything I find out, Poppy."

Margaret eased herself out of the apartment. The doorman downstairs was still somnolent.

"Detecting is expensive," she said to herself as she caught another cab. Then she said aloud, "When Helene and Istvan were precisely *what* centuries ago?" But of course she knew the answer.

The driver, a native of the Ukraine without a solid grasp of English, did not pay her any attention, concentrating on hurtling his cab through Central Park to Basil's West Side apartment.

Basil's apartment building, of brownish stone further dulled by the accumulated city grime of many decades, boasted bay windows with white trim on the upper stories. Beyond the small foyer and a heavy, locked glass door, Margaret could make out a cavernous and dingy lobby. B. Jones in 3A was listed on the row of bells and mailboxes.

Margaret pressed the buzzer. There was long silence, and she pressed again.

Finally, through the speaker grill, Basil's voice sounded faint and tremulous.

"Who is it?"

"Margaret Priam."

Another long pause ensued. Then, "Come up." Basil sounded resigned to his fate. The heavy front door emitted a buzz, and Margaret pushed it open. No doormen here, either stupefied or alert. Merely a floor of scuffed marble, a large mirror over a rickety settee, so aged and silvered now that it gave back only a distorted reflection. The antique elevator at the far end was barely five feet square, and it moved Margaret haltingly upward to the third floor. She stepped out into a hallway that did not even remotely suggest the aesthetic and refined Basil. Hideous wallpaper and an equally hideous and threadbare patterned rug stretched in either direction. Then Margaret spotted a light oak door gleaming with varnish and brass and knew she had arrived at 3A.

The melodious bell summoned Basil, who unfastened chain locks and bars and hesitantly opened the door to her.

"The police have been here," he said at once. "I didn't know what to say. I told them everything last night. Truly. They were here early this morning. They asked all sorts of questions."

"Basil, no one could possibly suspect you of murdering Helene." Margaret mentally tallied all the reasons why one might well suspect him. In spite of Poppy's hint of a rumor that someone or other had gossiped about Basil and Helene as more than friends, he did not now resemble a potential bridegroom. He seemed to have shrunk from his plump and confident self, and his color, Margaret thought, was not good. She had thought of him as fiftyish. Today he looked much older.

He led her into a living room much at odds with the building in which it existed. The ceilings soared; the windows with elaborate, tasteful drapes were a shining expanse. There was a huge marble fireplace with an enormous baroque mirror above, polished chairs and comfortable sofas, little glass-topped tables holding silver boxes and objets d'art. The ceiling writhed with plaster garlands and a chandelier hung with hundreds of crystal drops shimmered overhead. Beneath Margaret's feet on the polished floors were excellent oriental rugs.

"A sherry, Lady Margaret?" She nodded. "This has been such a terrible day." Basil was distracted. "Since I saw you . . ." He paused delicately, contemplating a sherry glass before he poured.

Margaret saw his eyes flicker in her direction. He was waiting to hear if she would mention seeing him on Fifth

Avenue. Margaret decided that he would not know that she had.

"Terrible," Margaret agreed, and peered through the glass top of the table beside her. "What a lovely woman," she said. "Here in this miniature."

"My grandmother," Basil said. "She was quite the Boston beauty in her youth. The belle of Beacon Hill. I love these old things, the way things were done in the great old days. Society meant something then." He handed Margaret her sherry, and for a moment she wondered if it might be her last, laced with a drop of cyanide to halt her prying in its tracks. Where did one get cyanide? She ought to look it up.

"What can I do for you, Lady Margaret?"

Margaret was startled out of her consideration of the sources of cyanide. "I hated to intrude today," she said. "I know you're grieving for Helene." She sipped her sherry bravely.

"Grief, yes." Basil was aroused. "But for times long past. She was not kind to me at the end. The others had turned her against me. I confess that without her, I would not have the life I do, but to hint to her that I took advantage..." Basil mopped his brow with a snowy handkerchief. "What she said to me last night at the ball..." Margaret leaned forward expectantly to hear precisely what Helene had said. She was not to hear it.

"It was personal business, Lady Margaret, but you cannot imagine how it destroyed me." He paused. "But it was not I who was destroyed in the end, was it? She always overstepped even her boundaries. On the other hand, you must understand, Lady Margaret, that people like Helene must be judged by different standards. To be a leader in society, as she was, was something special."

Margaret had a sharp memory of De Vere suggesting that the social class to which Helene belonged felt itself above the law.

"She was not one of these"—Basil waved his hand—"these arrivistes who flocked to her charity balls. She was Old Money, thanks to Nayland. Nayland was as distinguished a man as one might name, but before that even, she traveled in superior circles. Why, she was even close to the Duke and Duchess of Windsor. She was even acquainted with my family. And she lowered herself by these specious causes and charity things to which anyone might come." Basil gestured widely again and embraced the phantoms who had populated the Harpennis Ball. "It made me ill, truly. I tried to keep it from happening."

Margaret wondered if his final solution had been death to the betrayer of her class. "Oh, I do understand," she said.

"You know what this city is like nowadays," Basil said. "Clothing designers and decorators and the like masquerading as one of us. As if they knew anything about society."

This Margaret did understand. Back home, there were rigid class distinctions and one knew who was who. If one chose a life-style at odds with one's class, everyone understood, but everyone still knew who was who. In New York, almost everyone was no one on Basil's scale, and everyone was trying to be someone. Helene had done the trying—and had succeeded—so long ago that she was firmly in the select circle that lived by different rules.

"But you haven't told me to what I owe the pleasure of your visit?" Basil looked at her expectantly, perhaps thinking that now Margaret would mention having seen him on Fifth Avenue.

Margaret suddenly felt stupid. That was why she was here, to find out what there might be linking him and Janine. She fell back on Belle Nagy as her weak excuse.

"Mrs. Nagy asked me to find out about her husband's show."

Basil's reaction startled her.

"That woman! She haunts us. There was no question of this so-called retrospective. None. That was absolutely settled before . . . before Helene died. Only Helene hated to hurt anyone's feelings."

In Margaret's recollections of the deceased Helene, there was no strong sense of charity toward the feelings of others, but she let Basil's perception pass unchallenged.

"Mrs. Nagy fancied she had claims," Basil said cryptically. "But I believe it's the *depth* of a friendship that matters, not the length."

"Quite so," she said. Poor jealous Basil.

"You should speak to Janine," Basil said. "She kept track of that sort of thing." As he spoke Janine's name, Basil gazed pointedly toward the chandelier, but his eyes flickered nervously in Margaret's direction. Still worried, perhaps, that Margaret had seen him attempting to rendezvous with Janine.

"You and Janine must be close," Margaret said tentatively.

"Colleagues in the foundation," Basil said, firmly distancing himself from Janine. "Allied in doing what was best for Helene in her work." Basil stood up. "I must keep an appointment shortly, I'm sorry to say."

"The whole business has been so dreadful," Margaret said.

"Do you think the police know who did it?" Basil asked. "They asked me so many questions about her friends, and what happened, but I couldn't help them a bit. Not a bit."

"Nor could I," Margaret said.

"They even spoke to you?"

"I was there. Paul and I. When you went to call the ambulance."

"Someone had to act responsibly." Basil was defensive. Margaret detected a tremor as he set down his sherry glass. Fear? His seething preoccupation with the betrayal of himself and Helene by the arrivistes? There was something wrong, but she couldn't quite place it.

"What did you tell them? Did they mention me?" he asked.

"Of course not," Margaret said. "Thank you for seeing me. The funeral . . .?"

"Monday. St. Bart's, naturally. It will be a shoddy affair," he added glumly. "Robert has no style. The only decent part will be the church."


"Finally," Margaret said when Paul answered his telephone. "Listen, love, I've found out all sorts of interesting things."

"Where are you?" Paul said. "It sounds like a ladies' luncheon."

"Oh, at Josephine's. She does nails and faces and things. Divine place. I decided I needed a quiet haven to gather my thoughts until De Vere collects me for dinner."

"It doesn't sound quiet to me." Paul had strong memories of going as a child with his mother to hair and beauty salons in Rome to sit and wait patiently while she was made gorgeous amidst chatter and gossip. He had been fed *gelato* at intervals by the girls while his mother's hair rose to new heights and her toenails blushed with new colors.

"First of all, did you see Janine Sheridan?" Margaret asked. "I saw her at Fifth when I was leaving Sara, and I'm certain she was trying to meet Basil. She wanted to give him some envelopes. When she saw me, she ran off to Harpennis House and crept in the back way. Then she left without the envelopes."

"I didn't see her," Paul said, "but she is said to have been in love with Nayland Harpennis for years. Nina is going with me to Morley's tonight, and she told me something. She remembers jewelry . . . a cuff link, perhaps.

Diamonds and turquoise, possibly attached to an arm handing Helene the sorbet."

"Diamond and turquoise cuff links? I'm sure I would remember that I'd seen them. Who would wear something like that?" Margaret said. "Although one sees some remarkable things nowadays. Sara expects to get the whole pot, by the way. She really loathed her mother-in-law. And Poppy hinted about some ancient involvement of Helene's with Belle Nagy's husband, and someone else told me . . . no, I'll save that. Basil believes people were turning Helene against him. Look at the time," Margaret said suddenly. "De Vere's due here in a few minutes to fetch me. Come to Kasparian's tomorrow, could you? I'll be there around ten. Dare I bring De Vere to Morley's this evening?"

"I think not, " Paul said, and imagined the consternation if Margaret showed up on the arm of a policeman. "And I don't believe having him as my roommate is a good idea."

"Perhaps you're right," Margaret said. "He probably knows characters even more unsavory than the ones we socialize with."

"Be serious," Paul said.

"I'm very serious," Margaret said. "Really. Find out anything you can from Morley. You can tell me tomorrow, and I'll tell you what De Vere's first name is."

# Chapter 10

*In another* acceptable part of the city, tailored to a degree surpassing the dreams of John Weitz, Morley Manton drew himself up to his impressive six feet, five inches and announced to the foreman of a competent firm of building contractors that a doorway in a client's apartment under renovation was to be moved one inch to the left of where it had been for some forty years.

When the foreman protested mildly, Morley narrowed his very blue eyes, and in the end, it was arranged that the doorway be moved and the foreman not be fired. Morley brooked no denials of his aesthetic judgments. Since Morley's dearest friends in the world, who were all people who truly mattered, insisted that he was the best interior designer now living, Morley prevailed.

With that matter satisfactorily disposed of, Morley paused to place a few business calls.

One call was to a congenitally hysterical client whose astrologer had advised her against blue for her new dining room. Morley soothed her, drawing on the reserves of charm he carefully preserved for clients. Another call was to the caterer supplying the hors d'oeuvres for his cocktail party. Numerous sudden acceptances required many additional trays of tiny puff pastries filled with mashed-up tuna and charged for as if it were salmon, and a few more white radishes and carrots tortured into the unnatural shapes his guests seemed to enjoy. The cost of the parsley alone for garnishing the trays was staggering. Morley thought it a pity that sushi was no longer the nibble of the day. So neat, convenient, and pretty. The caterer suggested a foray into edible flowers, a hot California concept. Morley hesitated: a little too trendy for his guests perhaps.

"Why not?" he said finally. "It won't kill them."

Then a call placed to a phone booth on a corner a few blocks north of 125th Street, in a neighborhood where he had only once ventured in person.

"I don't know what will happen now," he told the person who spoke from the phone booth. "I'll know in a few days, but the police will sustain their reputation for incompetence. Nothing will be discovered. It will be deemed an accident."

The policeman who had interviewed him the previous night had not struck him as grossly incompetent per se, but Morley judged that everything he might be guilty of had been more than adequately obscured.

"What?" The other party was having difficulty making his way through Morley's phrasing. "Yes, that's what I said—they'll give up on the dude that did it."

Almost as an afterthought, Morley added, "I wonder if you'd care to come downtown tomorrow night to do a small job for me? You can leave it in the usual way. No, you won't be seeing anyone there. After this, though, we may have to change our procedure."

When he hung up, Morley was quite satisfied that Helene's death would not alter his life-style.

Ever since he had achieved Helene's confidence when Nayland's millions had been dumped in her lap, Morley had established comfortable and profitable relations with the Harpennis Foundation. Adjuvant Youth's program of giving the disadvantaged jobs planting flowers to beautify dismal neighborhoods far uptown had been a brilliant stroke on his part. If the flowers failed to survive long, at least the thought was kind. Helene had no idea that a geranium could cost so little, so she never hesitated to authorize payment of the hefty invoices from the Garcia Sisters Nurseries (the address a post-office box number). She certainly never knew that the Garcia Sisters and Morley Manton were one and the same. That was the least of the ways Adjuvant Youth were immensely useful to him. Moreover, they asked no questions.

Relations with the foundation could be expected to continue, since he had devoted considerable attention to ingratiating himself with Robert and Sara. A room in the de Bouvet Paris apartment decorated at cost. The arrangement with Boggel Brothers to consider the advantages of adding Bouvet-aux-Panaises vintages to their line. Invitations to private parties that boasted Jackie and Brooke Astor and the Trumps. Just this week, a little help to Sara in arranging a rendezvous with a man she fancied, although Morley could not for the life of him see the attraction. Personal introductions for her to the best haute couture designers, Nancy's hairdresser, some eminent maître d's.

It would all pay off in consideration from Robert when he inherited the running of the foundation. Sara was less grateful, but Morley could manage her. An intimate little relationship, perhaps, that would delicately balance Sara's greed for the accoutrements of wealth and his own ambitions for first-rank social acceptance. It was not so farfetched: an astutely publicized heterosexual flirtation to contribute to his social standing. Morley tested his nerves, and found he was calm. He was too clever to have anything to fear.

Morley Manton had checked every angle and was satis-

fied, a man for whom trompe l'oeil and faux alligator held
no terrors.


Belle Nagy sat most of the day in her large but shabby
apartment across the river from Manhattan, not far from
the Queens Midtown Tunnel. Outside, the rows of relent-
lessly brown buildings faced the spectacular Manhattan
skyline. Inside, she was surrounded by the huge, bright,
intricate paintings that were her only inheritance from Istvan. Helene had remarked on her one recent (brief) visit to
her friend's home that it was a pity Istvan's artistic vision
seemed better suited for rooms the dimensions of an audi-
torium rather than the modest homes most people fancied
nowadays.

"The impact," Helene said as she fled to a car she had
kept waiting during her visit, "is quite sensational. Was
that purplish thing really meant to be a palm tree? Rather
large. I always thought of Istvan as more . . . intimate.
Didn't he do simpler things years ago when you first settled here? Bridge builders with muscles and women with
head scarves?"

Belle always believed that the vivid blues and purples
and reds, and the semiabstract nature of Istvan's work,
were too advanced for Helene, who preferred dainty pastel
landscapes and still lifes of flowers and fruit painted by
very famous artists.

Belle was very tired today after the ball, but calm. The
police detective had offered a car to take her home, but she
had refused. Her neighbors were too interested in others'
business. After she had made the long subway ride home,
she had not slept well. She had kept seeing the body of her
old friend sprawled across the table, and feeling the impact
of sudden death, even though it was richly deserved.

"You know I could have killed her years ago," Belle

said to the spirit of the long-vanished Istvan. He was represented in today's one-sided conversation by the remarkably distorted portrait (so-called) of (possibly) a woman who was (probably) one of Istvan's casual mistress/models from his semi-cubist period. The one with the oddly shaped nose that alone of her features had survived the artist's personal vision of feminine beauty.

"I was there as a friend for her all those years; I gave up what was rightly mine because she said it meant her very life."

Belle's large gray and white cat opened an eye at the sound of her voice. Silver the cat was accustomed to the monologues and did not hear the pain or sadness in them. Since they did not portend food or games, he went back to sleep.

Belle had indulged in rambling conversations with Istvan since he had departed from her life thirty years before, slipping under the barriers back into the land he had emigrated from decades before. She had to imagine his responses, as she imagined his reappearance someday, looking just as he had when he had disappeared from her life.

"*Sweetheart, you must be patient.*" His voice was so clear, even in her head. "*Helene is a busy woman. But a true friend . . . Sweetheart, I have no feeling for her except for what she can do for us. We do what she asks, and she will repay us.*"

Belle stood up and walked through the apartment to the north-facing room where Istvan used to paint, where his easel with an unfinished canvas still stood, and all his pots and brushes and the glass plate where he ground his colors. His oils and brushes and knives were there, and the burner where he heated strange substances to make pigments, a true craftsman who did not rely on commercial colors. She had moved very little in all that time, only replacing what time had decayed, so all would be ready if Istvan returned. She did believe he would return.

"A show, Istvan," she said aloud. "With rich people to buy your work and critics to write about you and make you famous. And the fame will give me a fortune to keep me safe for the long years of waiting."

Belle sat down at Istvan's table and picked at the splintery surface with the old palette knife he had owned since turning his back on Transylvanian forests and setting out for New York so many decades ago.

Belle tried once again to reach Janine Sheridan at Harpennis House, and finally Janine answered. Belle could not say that she received satisfaction from the call. But there was always Robert. Now that Helene was gone, Robert could not refuse her.

Morley stretched out his lanky frame in the most comfortable chair in Poppy's boudoir. It was not a room he had decorated, and he disapproved of the frills and mushy cushions, the lacy curtains and the unbridled satin. "Well, dear, who do you suppose did it?"

Poppy chewed her lip and thought. "Not you, was it?" Morley shook his head. "I thought you'd say no. I asked Lady Margaret when she stopped by. She didn't know. Robert is likely, don't you think? Naturally Basil thinks the police are onto him."

"About what? Surely they don't think he did Helene in." Morley laughed. "Helene was his reason for existing, which is more than I can say about others. Don't look at me with that suspicious eye, Poppy darling. I don't know a thing about Helene's death, although I warned her often enough not to have those hoodlums in her house."

"Morley, Morley," Poppy said. "I know perfectly well you encouraged Helene to pour all that money into Adjuvant Youth, and I know why. I believe Helene was onto you."

"Was she indeed?" Morley sat up, tall and elegant. "I won't dignify your suggestion by asking what you think you know. More important, I could use a little item in 'Social Scene' about my party tonight. It's going to cost a small fortune with all these sensation seekers coming, so I might as well get some good out of it. One of my mixed-bag get-togethers. The arts and society, the madcap and the merely mad. They seem to enjoy mixing for brief periods. I've decided the fete will be in honor of that sweet Prince Paul Castrocani."

"You know he's Carolyn Hoopes's boy, don't you? I remember his father well. The family is old and excellent, but Aldo's probably still flat busted. I understand the boy is as attractive as the father. I'll see what I can do. Next week perhaps, when we see how all this murder business works out. I'd hate to be promoting someone on the way to the gallows. No, I don't mean Paul, dear." She smiled smugly and settled into her pillows.

"I can't imagine whom you do mean."

"Oh, probably not you. Your rise to eminence in your chosen field has not been without its murderous overtones, but I do not see you actually committing a murder for any of the usual reasons—revenge or money. Passion would certainly not be a viable possibility. Of course there are certain facts about your past of which I am aware but will naturally never reveal. However, that is not to say that others don't know them as well. Perhaps even Helene knew them."

Morley laughed. "I've outgrown my 'past.' It cannot harm me now."

"Now that Helene is dead?"

"That is not what I mean," Morley said.

"What of the present, then?"

"As you say, Helene is dead. The present does not trouble me either."

"I like your confidence, Morley. It is probably what makes it possible for you to deal successfully with those overbred and overrich women who find peculiar solace in a Manton-decorated room."

"They are extremely happy in my rooms," he said. "They know they are because I charge them so much. I do wish you'd let me make you happy by redoing this place."

"Run along, Morley," she said. "All this is very tiring. I do have important things to do. A newswoman is always on the job."

The phone beside her bed rang. Poppy waved Morley from her room and answered. "Yes, yes," she was overheard to say. "Of course." Poppy listened intently. "Ahha," she said.

Poppy caught sight of Morley lingering at the door to listen, and she scowled. He retired hastily.

"I'd be glad to see you," Poppy said to her caller. "I appreciate your confidence. . . . I do understand that your future depends on sharing your secrets with someone you can trust."

Poppy did not mention that there were few secrets she did not already possess.

Poppy waited until she heard Morley's heels clicking across her foyer and the sound of the door closing.

"I can't promise anything, but we'll see. Telephone me when you have the documents you mentioned."

When she hung up, Poppy lay back and closed her eyes. Helene's murder had stirred up too many memories. She mulled over fragments of old knowledge and bits of speculation mostly forgotten by everyone but her. She was mildly exhilarated by the thought that she was a journalist on the trail of the big story. She would shortly have concrete information that no one else possessed.

* * *

History does not record De Vere's thoughts when he reached the top of three steep flights of stairs and entered Josephine's establishment.

Margaret was waiting for the last dab of brilliant red nail enamel to dry when he appeared in this place of mirrors reflecting and re-reflecting the unlined faces of well-coiffed women with pampered hands that did not labor overmuch. He met a heady cloud of mingled scents—expensive perfumes, nail polish, softeners, hardeners, creams and unguents, and the aroma of rich brewed coffee. It was a clean, white place with touches of deep maroon and wicker chairs and couches with plump cushions.

The few remaining clients looked up at De Vere, curious for a moment, then returned to their gossip about messy divorces, lost loves, wayward husbands, and ungrateful children.

"De Vere, come sit with me until I've finished," Margaret said. "The day has been too depressing, so I decided to repair to the comforts of Josephine. It's one of my secret vices, the kind you spend money on no matter what. This is Josephine herself. Josephine, my friend Mr. De Vere, the detective."

A delicate beige woman with dark hair drawn back sleekly nodded and bent over Margaret's hand.

"I think Mr. De Vere finds the surroundings unsettling," Josephine said. "Would you like us to send out for something to drink while Lady Margaret finishes? Please do sit down."

De Vere sat on the edge of a wicker settee and scowled.

"I won't be but a few minutes," Margaret said sweetly. "I love to come here, so restful, no stress. I hope you don't mind."

"No," he said. "I don't mind meeting you, but if Josephine will forgive me for saying so, I hate this sort of place a lot."

Josephine laughed softly. "I thought policemen had to be at ease anywhere, since they must go everywhere in pursuit of evildoers."

"We do go everywhere," De Vere said, "but professionally, the question of being at ease doesn't arise. I believe I'll be genuinely at ease waiting for Lady Margaret downstairs. There is a bar in the restaurant at street level."

"Oh," Margaret said, "I thought you'd want to hear what Josephine has to say about Mrs. Harpennis. She was an occasional client here."

"No, no," Josephine said hastily. "I have nothing to contribute. She was a very pleasant lady. I merely mentioned to Margaret that she told me she had once visited the island in the Caribbean where I was born. 'An old amour and I took a holiday there many years ago,' she told me, 'because he liked to paint the sky over the Caribbean when the sun was just coming up. And he liked the way the colors of the crimson and orange bougainvillea made a . . . tropical statement.'" Josephine shrugged. "That was all. Mrs. Harpennis must have found the island quite primitive for her tastes if it was long ago."

"I wondered to whom she was referring," Margaret said disingenuously. "It must have been long before she married Nayland Harpennis. Of course, everyone knows about Helene's affairs. Sara thinks they've come back to haunt her. Kill her."

De Vere looked at her sternly. "According to informants, Mrs. Harpennis had a number of admirers over the years, but there is no indication that they played a role in her death."

Margaret shrugged. "Sara's spitefulness always goes beyond the bounds of acceptable behavior."

De Vere stood up. "When you're finished, I plan to take you to a place which I find restful, without stress. It will be an interesting contrast." He nodded graciously to Josephine, ignored the eyes that followed him, and departed.

Margaret watched him leave. De Vere appeared not to be aware of Istvan Nagy, so Helene's romantic idyll in the Caribbean had no significance. It seemed to prove that he was not much of a detective when it came to the lives of society's movers. No wonder he needed her help. Margaret smiled to herself. She decided she would take him someplace that would make this evening even more entertaining than he had planned.

"Josephine, an enormous favor, please."

Josephine glided across the room, slim and straight, looking like a delicate wisp of tropical sunshine.

"I've just decided to drop in at a sort of party. I don't have time to change, but a sort of dramatic makeup . . ."

Josephine chuckled. "That policeman is in for trouble," she said. She put a finger under Margaret's chin. "Some good eyes will do it. And I have some of my jewelry here. It's different."

Margaret like what she saw when Josephine had finished. The chunky, primitive gold necklace and long earrings elevated her brown-for-condolences dress to a another plane.

"I like it," Margaret said. "It's going to give me a lead in the contest of wills with Mr. De Vere."

# Chapter 11

*P*aul *was* relieved to discover that Morley had succumbed to a different trend and eliminated the excruciating chrome and glass from his apartment. It was now Southwestern—rough whitewashed walls and red tiles, colorful woven Indian rugs, and drab bits of broken pottery displayed in backlit cases as though they were priceless artifacts. A very large wrought-iron chandelier dangled from the ceiling, which someone had contrived to look as though it were made of heavy dark beams. No one in the crowded room risked standing directly beneath the chandelier.

Paul and Nina stood at the head of the short flight of stairs down into the sunken living room and caught the attention of several interested guests. Paul had to admit that Nina looked exceptionally pretty and refreshed in spite of the day's ordeal.

Morley, towering over the others, detached himself from his conversational group. He raised an eyebrow at the sight of Nina.

"How good you could come, Paul. And Nina dear, how pretty you look tonight. Won't everyone be delighted that two more witnesses to last night's events are here to regale us."

"Oh, no . . ." Nina said under her breath to Paul.

"There are dozens here eager to meet you." Morley walked ahead and expected them to follow. He was wearing a magenta Thai silk shirt and red silk trousers. He had underdressed for his at-home gathering.

Paul shrugged as if to tell Nina, "You know what Morley is like."

"Here is our guest of honor," Morley announced. "Prince Paul Castrocani, new to New York and soon to be dear to our hearts. Everyone, come here and meet Paul Castrocani . . . and Miss . . . Um."

"I'm not really the guest of—" Paul said.

"Of course you are," Morely said. "Here's Alex Whim, the writer. You've seen his things in *Vanity Fair*. That's the one, isn't it, Alex?" A rotund and hairy person shook his head no. Morley carried on. "Just nod here to Dr. Jungfrau. He's totally deaf, but he does love a party. Chat with my friends while I see what the help are up to in the kitchen. Probably eating my caviar by the spoonful. The bar is over there."

"What's the story?" Alex Whim the writer asked. Dr. Jungfrau beamed benignly and appeared to be lip-reading.

"Story?"

"I read that you were at the Harpennis charity thing where the murder took place."

"I know nothing," Paul said. "Nor does Nina."

"Pity. Morley had almost persuaded me to profile Sara de Bouvet for *International Woman*, but a scandal like this is bad. When it's long in the past, you can glamorize it. I was thinking I'd try a different angle. An exposé of society. Daughter-in-law murders for money. You know the sort of thing."

A very tiny, very ancient lady wearing centuries of makeup peered up at Paul. She had been listening to every word.

"I never liked him. Never trusted him. Never," she said firmly.

"Who?" Paul was bewildered.

"The Jones boy. I know he stole a silver spoon from me years ago. And probably sold it. It's a short step from there to murder. Mark my words."

"Psychologically speaking, I judge it rather to be a case of the son as victim striking back at the mother, his oppressor." Dr. Jungfrau pronounced his opinion in a booming voice. He might be deaf, but he was certainly not mute.

"I do not believe anyone knows who—" Paul began.

Dr. Jungfrau did not pause. "It is much more common than believed. Always the son is said to be in love with the mother, but I have found this is not the case. Hate. That is the emotion on which we build our fantasies."

"Now just a second, Jungfrau." Alex Whim placed himself in front of the doctor and spoke loudly into his face.

Nina nudged Paul rather forcefully and indicated the door with a nod of her head.

*"Dio!"* Paul winced.

"A problem?" Alex Whim surveyed the room.

"Not at all," Paul said. "Nina, would you excuse me for a moment?"

Margaret had just entered, and lagging behind her with a pronounced scowl was De Vere. In seconds, Paul was at her side. De Vere did not seem eager to commit himself to entering the apartment.

"What are you doing here, Margaret? We agreed it would not be a good idea." Paul hoped his nod to De Vere looked cordial.

"Don't sound so frantic, love," Margaret said. "De Vere told us he wanted to get a line on our kind."

"He will hear terrible gossip."

"He will handle it. Run along and take care of Nina."

Paul passed Morley, who was heading for Margaret.

"We seem to be welcoming the cops." Morley said to Paul as he passed. "Not your doing, I hope." He was at the side of Margaret and De Vere before Paul could deny it.

"Lady Margaret, what an angel to take the time. And . . . um . . . Detective . . . ? I'm afraid I don't recall the name."

De Vere, not a short man, had to look up to meet Morley's cold eye. "The name is De Vere," he said. "I am not on duty." He glanced around the room with barely concealed distaste. "Lady Margaret wished to put in an appearance."

"Then how good of you to accompany her. Not on duty, you say?" Morley raised an eyebrow.

"He's not here in an official capacity. I am . . . under Detective De Vere's protection because . . . well, leave it at that."

Morley appeared to survey De Vere's potential as a bodyguard. "You're not telling tales to the police about us, Margaret?"

"We are here merely for the pleasure of your party."

"Then let me introduce you and Detective De Vere to a few interesting people." Morley spoke with something like glee as he maneuvered them expertly into the room. "This is Barbie Twine. A *very* interesting person."

The middle-aged woman he indicated looked like a walking thrift shop, covered with fringed shawls and several skirts of different lengths. She batted her lashes, which were decked with silver mascara.

"I am in jewelry," Barbie said, and thrust out her hands. "See, I make it." She had extraordinarily long fingers, which was fortunate, since each one was burdened with immense chunks of metal studded with bits of polished rocks. Bracelets covered her arms to the elbow. "It is a highly specialized talent," she said. "I love your necklace," she said to Margaret. "Did I hear Morley right, you're some kind of lady?"

"Yes," Margaret said. "A perfect lady, and Mr. De Vere is a perfect gentleman."

"Ah," said Barbie, and clanked noisily as she pulled her shawls about her, disturbing the pounds of chains and pendants she wore about her neck. "You were at that thing last night where the old dame was killed off? I met her once. A bad bit of work."

"Ummm . . ." Margaret hesitated.

"Morley told everyone about it. He said the gang of thugs did it because the old girl was going to cut off their funds to buy dope, but that's ridiculous. Ho, boy!" This to a waiter passing among the guests with a tray of tiny mushroom caps stuffed with an unkown substance and artfully arranged on a tray. She took five.

"My personal view is that Morley did it himself. He's always displayed antisocial behavior, and he doesn't like being denied. He told me he was going to be a—what do you call it? Trustee of that foundation. Then I think she must have changed her mind so he knocked her off. Simple, huh?"

"Simplicity itself," De Vere said. "If you would excuse us for a moment, Lady Margaret and I will get ourselves drinks."

He took Margaret firmly by the arm and guided her through the crowd to a bar set up beside what turned out to be a fake fireplace built Southwestern style into a corner and crammed with mesquite logs.

"Perfect gentleman," De Vere muttered.

"I thought you'd find this amusing," Margaret said.

"As a matter of fact, I do. Especially what Barbie just said about Morley expecting to be named a trustee. I was under the impression it was Basil Jones who was expected to be named."

"How did you know that?"

"The police have their ways," De Vere said, rather more good-humoredly than Margaret had any right to expect.

"Poor Basil," she said. "He's in a terrible state because of this murder. I happened to . . . run into him."

"What about poor Basil?" Morley was back at their sides. "I'm sure he's bemoaning the fact that he can't have Helene lie in state in Harpennis House surrounded by miles of black velvet and six-foot candlesticks. A tasteful wreath of white roses at her feet as the faithful file by, with himself as chief mourner."

Margaret eyed Morley warily. Behind his sarcasm was a hint of real anger.

Then he smiled and took De Vere by the arm. "I wax wroth about Mr. Jones. He tends to blather about matters he knows nothing of to people who misunderstand. It is a personal thing. He was not a fit companion for Helene, but her eyes were beginning to be opened right at the end. Oops, I should not be gossiping with the police, should I?"

In quick succession, Margaret and De Vere were introduced to a sturdy man with an impenetrable accent who was a Czechoslovakian movie director; a lady of society who did not seem at all well nourished and who talked about her new career as a fashion designer ("Ruffles and more ruffles, ruffles to die over"); a glamorous couple, he in black tie ("We're going on to Bunkie's later") who turned out to be Broadway producers eager to discuss their new musical based on the life of Margaret Mead; and a prominent actress who succinctly and vulgarly stated her opinion of the producing couple. There was a blur of others gabbling and gobbling hors d'oeuvres. Only a tweedy pipe smoker, who looked to be a harmless enough woman, bothered to ask De Vere his profession and seemed genuinely interested that he was a policeman.

Paul and Nina drifted by with the look of imminent departure about them.

"We are leaving," Paul said. "Morley is more than we

wish to deal with tonight. Nina and I are going out to dinner."

Even as he spoke, however, Paul saw that he did not want to leave at once. Leila Parkins had appeared on the landing above the living room, surrounded by her coterie. "Chat with Margaret for a bit," Paul said to Nina. "I'll be right back." He made his way toward Leila. On the way he was accosted by a boy who asked him what his drug of choice was these days.

"Money," Paul said absently. "Excuse me."

There were others heading for Leila, but Paul reached her first as she surveyed the crush and waved to friends at the other side of the room.

"Hello, Leila," Paul said.

"Paul. I didn't know you mingled with Morley's set. I was going to call you. You remember Cummings Black? Cummy, fetch me a little something. A splash of wine." Cummings Black III surged away at her command. Leila had the makings of a Helene.

"Call me?" Paul was pleased. She took his arm and dragged him to a corner away from the others.

"Listen," Leila said. "Can I trust you?" Paul nodded emphatically. "What happened after I left the ball? Besides the murder. Did anyone mention me? Everybody's been telling me things, and I don't believe a word Morley says." Leila was especially bright-eyed and sparkling tonight and suspiciously cordial to him. He wondered if it were her deeply buried natural goodness showing through at last or the result of recent intake of a controlled substance.

"Margaret Priam and I were across the ballroom when it happened. I don't have much to tell." He was desperate to think of something that would hold Leila's fragile interest. "As far as I know, your name didn't come up. Of course, your name was on the guest list, so it's possible the police will contact you along with everyone else."

"They have. I mean, there was a message with my service. I haven't called back. Anyhow, I was already gone by the time it happened."

"It was a tragic thing," Paul said.

"Oh, screw the old bitch," Leila said. "She was always after me to be on her stupid committees and show up at those deadly affairs."

She seemed unconscious of the appropriateness of her comment.

"The worst was, she was always sending Basil Jones around to 'guide and inform' me. He tried to educate me, can you imagine? Take me to museums and places like that. We have some lovely pictures in Mummy's house that I can look at anytime I want. I don't need to walk around looking at things painted by some boring dead Italian. Ooooh, I forgot. You're Italian, aren't you? I mean really dead. A long time. Live Italians are sexy."

Paul took comfort in that, all the while wondering what it was she wanted from him.

"Basil didn't say anything about me, did he?" she asked.

"No. We barely spoke." Somewhere in the back of Paul's mind, he had a vision of Margaret firmly urging him on to find more clues, the better to impress Detective De Vere, who even now lurked somewhere behind the pile of mesquite logs.

"Basil was with Mrs. Harpennis when it happened," Paul said. "He ran downstairs to call an ambulance in the office."

"I see." Some sort of slow thought process was taking place in Leila's brain. "Well, of course he didn't make a call."

"He didn't?"

"When I left with Cummy and Gus, I forgot something in the coatroom. We got a cab and everything and were halfway where we were going and we had to turn right around and come back. We made the cab wait while I ran in. There's a public phone in the coatroom you know, and this waiter was speaking to the ambulance people on the phone. Then I saw Basil plunge downstairs through everybody and go into one of the offices and come right out. I thought it was funny. If he said he called, he was lying. He didn't have time to make a call. Then he went running back upstairs."

It seemed funny to Paul, too, and he felt a sudden clutch of panic at the possibility of a real clue that he might actually have to report to someone. He began to wish he had a notebook in the style of De Vere's partner Bergen in order to keep everything straight.

"You wouldn't know if Basil has cuff links made of turquoise and diamonds?" he asked and felt he was making immense strides as a detective.

"He has a lot of wimpy jewelry he likes to show off, old rings and pins and chains, but I shouldn't think even Basil would go so far as turquoise and diamonds. What does that have to do with anything?"

"They sound attractive," Paul said. "I might purchase something like them."

Leila looked at him as though he had suggested rounding off his wardrobe at K Mart.

"Please don't," she said. "Promise."

"I appreciate your interest."

"Leila . . ." Cummings Black III, with a dewy glass of wine, had been waiting patiently in the wings but was growing restive. "Morley wants you."

Leila silenced him with a look.

"What I really want to know," she said to Paul, "was who did it? I mean, I know all those people, and I know all sorts of things about them . . . Morley and Basil and the rest, and Mummy knows all the old ones, Mrs. Harpennis and Goneril and that horrid Countess Cloissoné. She's told me all about them. Like Robert's father wasn't really his father, because Helene was always fooling around, and how the countess used to be a hooker, and how Peter Pomfrette changed his sex from being Paula. I don't want to end up talking to the police about any of them."

"I understand," Paul said soothingly. "Don't worry. You had left the party by the time it happened."

"What about Basil?" she asked. "I can't get him in trouble, boring old thing that he is."

"If the police speak to you, you'll have to tell them, but I doubt that you'll hear from them again soon." Paul wondered if by his advice he was obstructing justice. He needed to consult Margaret, but he definitely didn't want to involve De Vere.

"That's a load off my mind," Leila said. Paul did not think her mind was overburdened at any time. "I've got to speak to Morley. Then we're going to dash."

Leila headed straight for Morley with Cummings Black III and Prince Gustav von und zu Lehrenmacht in her wake. The crowd parted obediently to allow her a path.

Paul searched the packed room for Margaret. She was chatting with a florid gentleman whom Paul recognized as someone famous but couldn't identify. De Vere was not in evidence.

"Margaret," Paul murmured. "A clue."

She abandoned her conversational partner graciously and pulled Paul to a comparatively quiet corner. "Tell me."

He told her what Leila had reported about Basil and the alleged phone call.

"He was very quick down and back again," Margaret said thoughtfully. "Hiding something? There was surely no murder weapon per se. Still . . . Keep it quiet for the moment. I'll speak to De Vere. Actually I'd better find him before he arrests the entire party on the grounds of arrogance and obnoxiousness."

Paul felt only mildly guilty when he returned to Nina. She was engaged in conversation with a very beautiful woman who turned out to be an expensive call girl whose apartment Morley had decorated.

"Leila's impending departure saves me from reminding you that I leave with the person I came with. The call girl did give me some interesting inside information on the sex life of the American urban male. Also foreign businessmen who end up lonely and alone in the city." Nina smiled sweetly. "Shall we go to dinner?"

"Please yes," Paul said.

As Paul held Nina's coat, he said, "Didn't you tell me that Basil spent a lot of time at Harpennis House?"

"Did I? He did. He shares Janine's office. Why?"

"Nothing. I suppose he'd use the back way when the house wasn't open for exhibits and things."

She started to say something, then stopped.

"He did then," Paul said.

"There is a back way," Nina said. "Janine sometimes uses it, too. It's frowned on, but there are some keys around. The caterer has been using it, but he'll leave his key when he finishes moving out the tables tonight. Why?"

"No reason," Paul said hastily. "It's just that Margaret saw Miss Sheridan disappear into an alley behind Harpennis House. I was simply curious about where she was going."

Suddenly Leila was at his side.

"We're leaving, Paul," she said, ignoring Nina. "Morley's friends are too boring, but I promised to pop in so he'd decorate my new little pied-à-terre for cost. I didn't realize he was giving this party for you. Poppy's writing it up."

"It's not for me," Paul said. "Until last night, I didn't even know there was a party, and until this afternoon, he didn't know I was coming."

"It doesn't matter. The publicity is super. Later we're all going downtown to that new club, The Nose Knows. They pipe in scents. The woman who gives parties at the clubs for tacky people is taking it over tonight. She begged me to come and I refused, so I thought I'd make her day and show up. Join up with us, won't you?"

Paul looked at Leila's perfectly painted lips, her adorable dimple, the golden ringlets cascading to her shoulders. Expensive from the tips of her dainty manicured toes to the top of her shining head. A family fortune behind her that boggled the mind. A dream come true.

He said bravely, "Nina, would you care to go? Leila, you must know Nina Parlons."

Nina smiled sweetly. "Leila and I have met several times. She gave generously of her time and talent for the Junior Committee. A visit to The Nose Knows sounds like fun."

The famous Parkins pout appeared on Leila's face for but an instant. "It's way downtown," she said. "Mention my name at the door." She departed with her entourage.

Paul and Nina lingered until she was well and truly gone and left themselves, just before Margaret and De Vere.

De Vere said to Margaret, "You've had your little game. I have behaved well. I even enjoyed my conversation with the pipe-smoking lady on the lesbian position on supply-side economics. Now we will leave this unspeakable place and worse people."

"They're not so bad," Margaret began. Then she said meekly, "I'm ready to leave. I'm starving."

"The food here is a little peculiar," De Vere said. "They're serving flowers. Not filling, but quite tasty. Let me see if I can match both food and ambience."

"You have no ticket," Margaret said when they reached his illegally parked car.

"One of the perks of being police," De Vere said. "One of the few."

*Chapter 12*

"*I*'ve *not* been much in this part of the city," Margaret said, and frowned at the Formica-topped table the very ancient Chinese waiter indicated. He appeared to recognize De Vere. There were some elaborate bits of plastic decoration here and there and long strips of pink paper with bold Chinese characters taped to the walls. A few middle-aged Chinese sat talking and smoking at a long back table piled high with empty dishes. Through the plate glass window, the teeming sidewalks of Chinatown were visible, and the neon signs on Mulberry and Mott streets were blinking and twinkling. The streets were packed with cars.

"In fact," she added, "I can't say that I've ever been here before. It's not a part of town where one often needs to be."

"Unless one wishes authentic and excellent Chinese food," De Vere said. He held a chair for her.

"There are some quite nice Chinese restaurants uptown in my neighborhood," she said. "And they seem to be in the hands of persons of the correct ethnic persuasion, so presumably the food is prepared by same."

"I thought we would be more likely to have a quiet dinner if we were not in the environment your set prefers.

133

And I hoped you would find Chinatown a delightful adventure. Right up there with murder and charity balls."

"As long as you mentioned it," Margaret said, "what is now known? Please don't tell me you're not at liberty to mention anything."

"I'm not, but there's very little to tell. As I predicted, no one knows anything. People are trying to trace the cyanide. Someone thought it might be a good idea to see if cyanide is used in insecticides in French vineyards."

"Aha! Robert. Of course! Or Sara. She could slip a pound of cyanide into her Louis Vuitton traveling case, and nobody would be the wiser. I paid a call on her this afternoon and came away convinced that she was capable of any manner of viciousness."

"Don't draw hasty conclusions," De Vere said, and added slyly, "Does your visit to Madame de Bouvet mean you are assisting the police?"

"Naturally not," Margaret said. "I was merely condoling. She had nothing to say except to imply that Helene's millions were now hers."

The old waiter, without waiting for an order, placed what looked like a long, pale white egg roll with a greenish filling before them, "Go on," De Vere said. "Fukien fish roll. It's good. Anyhow, cyanide is used for a number of purposes or as a component of various substances. It's not my field. I only mentioned the son and daughter-in-law because they seem the most deserving of police attention. Greed is a powerful motive, and I am the first to acknowledge the all-encompassing greed of the so-called upper classes."

"You would be manning the guillotine, then, comes the revolution?"

"I wouldn't go that far," he said, "but I do have certain reservations about your class. As a whole."

"I hope not about individuals, specifically." She looked across at him and continued to enjoy what she saw.

"Remains to be seen," De Vere said. "Ah, dim sum. They make them up after usual hours for me especially."

The waiter had returned with a number of steamers holding transparent dumplings, crispy bits of chicken, and puffy white balls of dough.

De Vere said, "You probably know dim sum. I understand they've moved uptown. These are the real thing. You might not care for the turnip cakes. My wife loathed them."

Margaret decided then that she would like them, however loathsome they might be. She plunged in, proud that even in uptown Chinese restaurants one learned to manage chopsticks.

"Is that why you divorced? Because your wife didn't like . . . these? They're delicious."

"No," he said seriously. "We divorced because being married to a policeman can make a woman crazy. Certain women anyhow. I liked her too much to allow her to spend her life being crazy. I come here often. I've had business in the Chinatown area from time to time. They are an interesting people, don't you think?"

De Vere smiled across the table, his chopsticks poised above the last dumpling.

Margaret looked at him, astonished. One might be introduced to Yo-Yo Ma or Ozawa, or speak to someone like Pearl at Pearl's Restaurant, or perhaps the Koreans who ran the vegetable store, or the occasional prosperous dealer in Chinese antiquities from Hong Kong who would visit Kasparian's shop, but one personally knew rather few Orientals.

"I know a little about their art," she said finally.

"Yes, you would," De Vere said.

"One moment," Margaret said. "I did study art and art history. I'm quite well educated for a social butterfly, which is, I presume, how you view me."

De Vere laughed. "Don't be so defensive. I'm sorry.

What else have you come up with in your attempt to assist the police?"

"Nothing."

"I'd like to think you'd tell me everything, Lady Margaret, but I am not such a dolt. Please keep in mind that if you do hear anything pertinent, it is your lawful duty to tell the police."

The vision of Janine scuttling back and forth between Harpennis House and Fifth Avenue clutching envelopes to her bosom almost made Margaret confess to De Vere. But she hesitated to cause trouble for Janine if she were innocent, and how could she be otherwise? Murdering Helene would have put an end to her career.

De Vere added offhandedly, "And it's your young prince's duty as well. Now, I don't know whether you'll enjoy what Mr. Lee is sending out to us, but it's excellent. It's called 'Happy Family,' but I believe the accurate translation is 'Prosperity to All in the Family.' It seemed appropriate in view of what I understand to be Sara de Bouvet's expectations." He dipped into the large earthenware casserole and held up a blackish piece of something. "You can skip the fish maw if you choose," he said. "I like the texture."

Margaret began to consume Happy Family with great relish, along with some especially delicious noodles. Then she stopped and closed her eyes.

"De Vere . . ."

"You've thought of something else?"

Margaret knew that she had to tell De Vere about Basil and the phone call, and yet she hesitated to bring trouble to that earnest, slightly silly man who had devoted so much time and effort to the comfort of Helene Harpennis.

"De Vere . . . do you have a Christian name?"

"Yes," he said. "What do you remember?"

Margaret took a deep breath. "Both Basil and a waiter claimed to be going downstairs to call an ambulance. At least that's what they told Paul and me when we were coming back to the ballroom to say good night to Helene and the murder happened. Basil went downstairs and returned so quickly, we wonder if he actually did make a call."

"Mr. Jones has offered a number of suggestions about the murder. We are aware of the waiter, who has not been located. He was a new employee of the catering firm, but with good references. An out-of-work actor. Your friend Dr. Mittman has stated that he did not seem murderous or otherwise crazed when he was sent to call for help. What might you be able to tell me about Mr. Jones?"

Margaret decided she couldn't do Basil any harm. "He was devoted to Helene, in the way that poor men with lavish tastes are devoted to very wealthy women. The history books are full of them."

"Not the books I am familiar with," De Vere said, "but I get your meaning."

"I don't know precisely what his background is. He's from a Boston family and hints that it was Beacon Hill society. I'm sure he went to a good preparatory school, a good university probably, with some sort of fine arts study, since he writes little articles about this and that. Not a scholar. Has never had much money. Cheap travel arranged so that no one notices, good clothes and distinguished jewelry he can ill afford, a rent-controlled apartment with a fairly good address. You find his sort around this city. By the way," she said as she snatched the last plump pink prawn on the plate before De Vere got it, "I don't suppose you really enjoy living in that hotel."

"Not especially. It's hard to find a place in Manhattan that doesn't cost the earth. I haven't had time to look in the other boroughs. The hotel is convenient."

"I had a thought," Margaret said cautiously. "About a place to live. Not my place," she added hastily.

"The thought never occurred to me," De Vere said. "Are

you getting enough to eat?" He watched her from the corner of his eye with a slight smile.

"Yes, certainly. About the apartment. It's a friend of mine. He has a place in Chelsea with an extra room and he'd like to share rent and utilities. A nice man. Responsible, working. Not gay or into drugs. It's reasonable. Are you interested?"

"To the extent that I wonder at you acting as a real-estate agent. What might your motives be?"

"I have no ulterior motive. Your work has made you suspicious. Do you suspect all women?"

"When I know you better, I may recount the story of my doomed marriage. Before then, such questions are prying."

"I don't mean to pry," she said defensively. "I was certainly not prying. Would you care to see the apartment? I could meet you there at eleven tomorrow and . . . introduce you. It could make your life easier."

"All right, I'll look. I'm getting tired of picking my way through the ladies of the night in the hotel's so-called lobby."

"Eleven it is." She wrote out Paul's address, leaving out his name. "The second-floor apartment." Paul had reluctantly surrendered that information. Presumably the police could determine who lived at any given address, but between now and tomorrow morning, De Vere might not have time.

"I hope I won't be dealing with the sort of person who haunts your charity balls and cocktail parties."

"Not a haunter," Margaret said. She was relieved that De Vere hadn't thought the information about Basil was worth pursuing. "He doesn't have money to spare for charities."

"I meant to ask you," De Vere said, "about the rationale of a ball such as the one last night. We know from Miss Parlons the costs involved and the number of tickets sold. The net profit is quite small. It seems scarcely enough to support the advertised activities of Adjuvant Youth. Wouldn't it be more efficient to ask people to contribute or to spend foundation money without the trouble of the ball?"

"Life is filling up time, don't you think? Some people have a lot of things to fill it with, working and doing the laundry and being in love. Others don't. A good many of the ladies at last night's ball, and hundreds of others like it, don't have much to do, because they have other people to do it for them, so a charity party gives them the chance to run things and have their way. Go shopping for dresses to wear, find a good hairdresser, gossip about it all afterward. Other people with a lot of money go in order to participate in a charitable cause."

"It allows them a tax deduction, and the opportunity to compare ball gowns." De Vere shook his head.

"It shows they aren't totally selfish," Margaret said.

"And it gets their names in the paper. Do you enjoy it?"

Margaret shrugged. "I can't really afford to keep up with them, but they are daffy about titles. It's the only life I know. Helping Adjuvant Youth can't be all bad."

"True, they aren't bad kids, even if people at their level of society live far more dangerous and violent and deprived lives than you could imagine. One or two of the present group have had brushes with the law. The Cruz boy, for one. But my current interest in them is peripheral. I am more interested in the activities of their sponsor—no, not Mrs. Harpennis. Mr. Manton, host of that alarming cocktail party. Do you know anything of him?"

Margaret sighed. "You know what high-powered interior designers are like."

"I can't say that I do."

"Morley is very social. A little tyrant with clients. Rather, a tall tyrant. He wants to have his work appear in every issue of *Architectural Digest*. He wants to be mentioned in the *Times* regularly. He wants to be in the col-

umns. He wants to know everybody and be invited everywhere. He'd like to be as famous as Donghia or Mario
Buatta. I don't know that he's talented or clever enough.
He couldn't be involved in anything that concerns the police." She stopped. "Yes, he could. There has been the odd
rumor. Drugs? Is that what you really do?"

"I wouldn't be able to tell you if that were the case," De
Vere said. "I was merely asked to check on a rumor that
came to someone's attention. Meeting him last night and
tonight added little to my knowledge, but considerably to
my private opinion."

"You asked us to help."

"I asked if you would let me know anything that might
shed some light. You aren't supposed to go plunging in,
clouding the evidence and terrorizing the suspects."

"You have suspects, besides Robert and Sara?"

"I did not say they were suspects. Nor is there a dangerous revolutionary on the horizon. All of Mrs. Harpennis's
friends who thought enough of her to remain behind last
night—Basil Jones, Miss Sheridan, Mrs. Nagy, even Morley Manton—do not seem like people prone to random
violence. Nevertheless, they were all there at the time.
People other than myself are examining possible motives
When I investigate such crimes of violence, I prefer solid
evidence to motives."

"De Vere . . ."

"Why don't you call me Sam?" he said.

She looked across the table at him speculatively. "I will
if you like," she said, "but that can't be your name. What
was it I was saying? Yes. Those people you mentioned.
They were not her friends."

"Oh? What were they?"

"As I recognized and Paul's mother pointed out, they
were her servants, as much as . . ." She would have mentioned Claire, but Claire would never speak to the police,
would probably take the first plane home to Switzerland if

they approached her, and Margaret wanted to hear what she had to say. "As much as a butler or a cleaning lady. They just wore prettier clothes and did her bidding on a first-name basis. In return, Basil has something like status in society, Janine has a job, Morley is in trade when you come right down to it, but is allowed to mingle with his customers on a social basis because of Helene and people like her, and because he's hot. Who else is there? Oh, Mrs. Nagy. She's some kind of old friend Helene threw delicious crumbs to. Servants." Margaret decided not to mention the ancient Istvan-Helene-Belle triangle, since Belle didn't seem to care after all these years.

"Very interesting," he said. "I wouldn't have seen that. I don't deal much in servants from a master's point of view, since I am a servant of the people myself."

"Remember that the master—mistress in Helene's case —has a responsibility to the servants," Margaret said. "The servants will turn on you if the responsibility is betrayed."

"I will keep that in mind," De Vere said. "Shall we go somewhere for a drink or walk after I make one phone call?"

"I hope you are providing your colleagues with all of my clues," Margaret said.

"Actually not. I wanted to tell someone I wouldn't be able to come around tonight."

De Vere told her no more, although she was curious to know. She wondered what sort of woman he liked. Somehow she had the impression that he was overlooking her British accent as a kindness, and her social class as an unfortunate accident of birth. He was being very nice about it.

Very late that night, the city as it always does awoke from a dinner-hour doze and put on its flimsy finery.

Chinatown continued to be ablaze with neon and packed with cars and walkers on the pavements. Greenwich Village, where Margaret and De Vere ended up for a drink, was bright and alive with the types who preferred the tangled streets of the Village to the straight Avenues farther uptown.

Paul and Nina found themselves at the unimpressive entrance of The Nose Knows, and then inside the gloriously impressive club with its dance floor that stretched for acres. Leila's name worked magic, and they lost themselves among mirrors and strobe lights, loud music and the wafting odors of Poison, Obsession, Big Macs, and pesto.

While Paul and Nina danced under the lights and Leila cut her own patented swath through people who surpassed Morley's guests by a wide margin in oddness of dress and life-style, far uptown at the darkened alley behind Harpennis House, a still figure watched the caterer's men carry tables and chairs out through the alley to a waiting van.

The lights in the house went off and the alley door slammed shut. As the van pulled away, the figure walked quickly down the alley, watched by others who were also observing the house from recessed doorways on the opposite side of the cross street.

Suddenly a single light came on again in the house, and a uniformed man leaned on the sill of a tall first-floor window on the south side of Harpennis House and scanned the street. The approaching figure halted, turned, and hurried away. A short time later, the other watchers slipped away into the night.

Ali Jackson had a very high rating with the security company that normally responded only if the front doors or windows of Harpennis House were breached and the alarm sounded.

Although he wasn't keen on guarding a house in which a murder had been committed, Ali was intrigued enough by the assignment to stay all night this once. He himself lived in Brooklyn with seven people in a three-and-a-half-room apartment. This was a rare opportunity to roam through Harpennis House and marvel at the amount of space that had once been deemed necessary for the comfort of a handful of human beings.

# Chapter 13

*W*hen *Paul* woke up on Saturday after barely four hours of sleep, he struggled upright and immediately ran through everything he had learned, and tried to remember what he had and had not reported to Margaret: Basil and the phone call he couldn't have made; Morley as a trustee; Basil as a trustee; Basil's space in Janine Sheridan's office; the cuff link; Janine's unrequited love for Nayland Harpennis.

He shuffled downstairs to the kitchen and boiled water for instant coffee, which he loathed. He was always forgetting to buy filters for the coffee maker. And coffee, for that matter. He hoped that the future roommate would be deeply committed to freshly brewed coffee.

*"Dio!"* What was it Leila had said? Robert's father not being really his? And the key to the alley doorway, left behind by the caterer in Nina's possession.

He was not equipped to deal with the implications of the information. He wasn't suited to living here under these circumstances. He belonged in a place where one rang for room service and one's desires were gratified immediately. If not immediately, then one complained to the manager.

Having reviewed his resentments, Paul showered,

shaved, and dressed, ready to present himself at Kasparian's shop.

The golden September of the past couple of days had seen fit to disapppear. The day was misty and damp, with a bleak cloud cover and streets slick from intermittent splashes of light rain. It was chilly. When cities turned mean like this, Paul had always headed south. Once he had gone as far as Kenya. Once he had even ended up in Australia.

The outside of Kasparian's shop was understated and tasteful: a small, deep display window with a single celadon vase, a heavy dark wooden door with a discreet brass plate reading B. KASPARIAN—ORIENTAL ART—BY APPOINTMENT.

Paul pushed the doorbell.

It was not Margaret and it could only have been Kasparian who opened the door and bowed him inside.

"I know from my experience with buyers in this market that you are not one, so you are therefore the Prince Paul whom Margaret is expecting. Bedros Kasparian." He held out his hand.

"Paul Castrocani. She admires you."

Kasparian, a foot shorter than Paul, shrugged and grinned. "A fine tribute from an astute woman. I admire her. She phoned to say that she is in pursuit of information from a maid. She will be here shortly."

Kasparian led Paul into the shop, which contained a few graceful chairs, a table or two, and a very beautiful Chinese oriental rug in pale blue, geranium, and cream. Examples of Kasparian's inventory were on display in individual glass cases—an ivory statue, an odd-looking three-legged pot that was ancient rather than artistic, an Imari plate, a jeweled dagger. At the far end of the shop was the only indication that this was a business establishment rather than a sparely but expensively furnished drawing room. A small desk with a vaguely Eastern appearance was piled with catalogs and invoices.

"Sit down," Kasparian said. "I have the coffee almost made in the back. You'll have a cup? Coffee is my specialty."

"Yes, please," Paul said.

Kasparian hurried off, saying over his shoulder, "If the doorbell rings and it is not a uniformed chauffeur with a limousine at the curb sheltering a customer, ignore it."

In moments he was back with excellent coffee that made Paul's at-home instant a shameful memory.

"I only know what I read in the papers," Kasparian said. He didn't sit but walked about the shop, pausing to admire his art-for-sale. "I am not morbidly interested in who killed Mrs. Harpennis, although I suspect it was for a reason both sordid and tragic. A little madness, a little revenge. Lovely, isn't it?" he murmured before a case that held an earthenware head of a horse with traces of brownish-red coloring. "Han dynasty. Very rare."

Paul noted the horse's fearsome wild eye and flaring nostrils.

"I have been in the art game for a good many years," Kasparian said. "Fifty perhaps." He shook his head. "Fifty years. All kinds of art, paintings, sculpture, fine rugs, you name it. This Basil Jones who was Mrs. Harpennis's friend. I know him, and how little he knows. The Manton person." Kasparian's tone indicated even less respect for Morley. "He buys from me occasionally for his clients, and would be perfectly willing to buy a fake piece at a low price and charge them as though it were the real thing. And of course, I knew Istvan Nagy and his wife years ago."

"Mrs. Nagy was at my table at dinner at the ball," Paul said.

"Yes, the wife. I used to visit them over in Queens when we were all much younger. Odd fellow, came here from

Hungary as a youth. Very attractive to women, while claiming to be dedicated to his art. The same might be said of Picasso. Too bad."

"Please?"

"Too bad, because unlike Picasso, Nagy was not capable of both womanizing and great art. He was not even a fairly good painter, although he took parts of the profession seriously. He claimed to follow assiduously what he insisted was the tradition of the artist, the true craftsman, preparing his own canvases, grinding his own colors. Creating pigments, that sort of thing. I had the sense that his devotion to the preparatory steps absolved him from the necessity of improving his work." Kasparian shrugged. "We all are guilty of avoiding challenges, although he apparently went off to face a different challenge from which he did not return."

"And so he died?"

"They say he went back to Hungary during the Revolution in the fifties, and disappeared. Perhaps he was escaping his failures in art and the burdens of a lifelong pursuit of women. Unfortunately, his work did not increase in monetary value or genius after his reported demise."

"Very interesting," Paul said politely.

Kasparian beamed at Paul. "He kept changing his style —abstract, cubist, you name it. Nothing worked. The wife was a childhood friend of Mrs. Harpennis's, although she was not then Mrs. Harpennis."

"Then you knew Helene long ago?"

"Mmm. Not to say know. A beauty, fascinating. She went off to England before the war, and then to France where she married de Bouvet, who was not as distinguished or rich as she thought he was. We met again not long ago, when she was securely wealthy at last, but she did not recall me. Or she no longer admitted to having shopkeepers as acquaintances, however successful. More coffee?"


As early as she dared on Saturday morning, Margaret called the Harpennis apartment and spoke to Claire.

"The butler told me of your offer of a place, but I cannot accept. I have made other arrangements," Claire said, and Margaret sensed a reluctance to continue the conversation.

"I wanted to speak with you on another matter as well," Margaret said. "You know that Mrs. Harpennis was a relative of mine." She wondered how long that story would hold up.

"I did not," Claire said.

"Distant. I hoped we could meet to discuss a question that troubles me."

"It is impossible." Claire's tone was wary.

"It is important. The information I seek will not be shared with anyone who could cause you trouble."

Claire remained reluctant, but in the end, Margaret's persuasive powers succeeded. Claire agreed to meet her at nine at a coffee shop on Madison, not far from Kasparian's shop.

"I must do an errand for . . ." Claire searched for a word to describe Sara. "For M. de Bouvet's wife." She was not running the errand with goodwill.

A little after nine, Claire arrived at the coffee shop. She accepted only coffee and seemed nervous as she awaited Margaret's questions.

"Aunt Helene seemed upset the night of the ball," Margaret said. "I wondered if she had been in poor health."

"Perfect health," Claire said too quickly, "although Madame was not as young as she seemed. Her . . . guests tired her, and I believe there was some little intrigue at the foundation which troubled her. Nothing more. Nothing."

Instantly Margaret knew there was something more.

She said gently, "Claire, if you know of anything that concerns her death . . ."

"I do not," Claire said firmly, but the nervousness remained. Margaret waited. Then Claire said, "I overheard M. de Bouvet and the lawyers speaking of an autopsy. Is this the case?"

"I don't know," Margaret said. "I presume it is the usual thing under these circumstances."

"Then they will discover if there were medications and such?"

"I have no idea, but why don't you tell me what it is that is troubling you."

Margaret heard then of the "tonic" provided by Claire's uncle, how it lifted Mrs. Harpennis from weariness and helped her move through her daily social round.

"I did not think it harmful," Claire said. "It could not have contributed to her death, but I have been worried that I . . ."

"Her death was caused by a dose of cyanide," Margaret said. She was recalling Helene's bright chatter, her sudden shift of mood, her unseemly display of anger in public. Poor Claire had probably been overdosing her with some form of amphetamine. Well, part of the fault lay with Helene in her determination not to be slowed by increasing age. Margaret had seen plenty of women—and men—in her circle take to mild or severe forms of drugs that helped to maintain the perfect facade. But the fact remained that Helene had not controlled her emotions, had perhaps spoken the wrong thing to the wrong person, which had perhaps triggered the violent act that killed her.

"If anything comes up," Margaret said, "you can be sure that I will see that you do not receive any blame."

The voice of assurance seemed to calm Claire. She relaxed, and Margaret pursued her advantage.

"I wonder if you could tell me anything Aunt Helene might have said about her . . . her attachments over the years."

Claire hesitated. "I was only with Madame for the past fifteen years. She was happily married to Mr. Harpennis, and grieved greatly when he died. She did not have what you call attachments during her marriage. What I could tell you would only be what she might have mentioned about the past, when I dressed her hair, for example. When she she felt the need to recall different, happier times, especially after Mr. Harpennis died. I did not witness the events, merely heard her stories."

"Hearsay. I understand."

"The son," Claire said softly. "Something troubled her about him. I believe that the father was not Madame's husband. I understand that this is not shocking in the circles Madame traveled." Claire's tight lips implied that it was indeed shocking to her Swiss sensibility, but it was not her place to say so.

"In truth," Claire said, "I am not sure that he was even Madame's natural son." Margaret held her breath while Claire looked down at her coffee cup. "I surmised this because of a telephone call I overheard some years ago. Madame spoke in anger. My English was not as good then as it has become, but I understood her to say that if M. de Bouvet—Robert, she said—had been her own flesh and blood he would have not have been so witless as to behave in thus and such a way. 'The blood is speaking,' she said, 'not the breeding I gave him.' It was some crisis, some foolish thing he had done about money perhaps."

"To whom might Mrs. Harpennis have been speaking?"

"I do not know." Margaret detected a hint of nervousness and thought that Claire had a good idea who it had been. "An intimate, I judge. It was very long ago. It cannot be significant now."

"Perhaps not," Margaret said casually. She did not wish to frighten Claire off. "I don't suppose Mrs. Harpennis had papers she kept carefully, documents or the like."

Claire smiled faintly for the first time. "While we still lived at Harpennis House, Madame kept a locked box in her boudoir. I do not know what it contained. I did not see it come with us to the new home. It may be that it is still at Harpennis House. She kept an office there." Claire stood up. "I must be returning."

"Thank you for speaking to me." Margaret hesitated, unsure how to phrase her next question. "Do you . . . do you have sufficient cash to get on for the moment?"

Margaret was fairly certain that Claire was a woman who socked away her earnings and probably had larger liquid assets than Margaret did. Still, a reward for information might be expected.

Claire shook her head. "It is kind of you to ask," she said, "but you need not pay for this information. I was very fond of Madame. I should like to see justice done, although I do not see that what I have told you can have any bearing on her death."

Claire departed in dignity, and Margaret pondered the secrets of expensive lives, which very likely did have a bearing on Helene's murder. She stepped out into a downpour that followed her to the shop. Kasparian and Paul were chatting comfortably.

"Ah, Margaret. I was explaining to Paul the difficulties of authenticating Renaissance paintings to the complete satisfaction of all the so-called impartial experts. And the financial rewards inherent in owning or purveying such art."

"The Castrocanis supposedly own a painting my father claims is by Raffaello," Paul said. "I do not believe it."

"We have a gallery back home full of things that are

supposed to be by someone or other," Margaret said. "The eighteen-century Priams pillaged the Continent on their Grand Tours. I never knew enough to say what was genuine and what wasn't. My brother has sold a few pictures to keep the Priory in repair, but he hates to get rid of anything. Well . . . have you had any new insights about our murder?"

Paul said, "I tried, but I don't believe I am very capable when it comes to detecting. An event takes place and seems to have a meaning, but I do not know how to fit it in."

"I am superfluous when it comes to murder," Kasparian said.

"That's what I mean," Paul said. "Not that you're superfluous, but that you have been telling me some interesting stories about Helene and the Nagys, tales of Basil and Morley, and I do not know where to fit them."

"An old man's reminiscences. Still, Nagy was a vivid character. A man who . . . who could not help but have an impact. He liked money. Even as far back as the Depression, when we were all struggling to survive, he boasted that he had an eye for long-term investments with a high rate of return. Perhaps he was convinced he would be able to fool some of the critics some of the time," Kasparian withdrew with a nod.

"I would not know a Nagy painting if I came face-to-face with it," Margaret said. "But if Kasparian said he was bad, he probably was."

"He was certainly an eccentric," Paul said. "He made his own paints and the like, and attracted women. Now I appreciate women—Margaret?"

She was gazing up at the ceiling with a frown. "What? I'm thinking of the long-term investments. Wait one moment." She went to the back to find Kasparian. Paul stood up and looked around at the pieces of the ancient East that had survived the tides of history to reach the shores of

Manhattan only to end up gracing the cabinet or wall of a penthouse overlooking the East River.

Margaret returned looking thoughtful.

"Has progress been made, do you think?" Paul was understandably anxious to disentangle himself from the murder.

"Yes," Margaret said. "I am pleased you had a talk with Kasparian. He knows a good deal more about art than anyone I can think of. He probably also has a very good idea who murdered Helene—without any proof, naturally—but he would not admit it. Is Nina at Harpennis House today?"

"Yes. She had to finalize some matters with Janine, and people are going to be there to see about hanging a new show in the gallery. Apparently the foundation goes on."

"Not good," Margaret said. "I'd like to take a look around when nobody's there."

Paul took a deep breath and was certain he would live to regret what he then said.

"Nina has a key to the back door."

"Perfect! Than you'll call her and say we need to borrow it tonight after everyone's gone."

"She'd never..."

"She would for you. Doesn't she like you? Didn't you have an enjoyable evening?"

"It was pleasant. We went to some clubs downtown. Since we became a part of Leila's party, it cost me very little. The club people seem to feel Leila and her followers are an expense they are happy to absorb. But I couldn't ask Nina..."

"It's important. It's murder. Hah! Look at the time. I have to see someone downtown in a while. Could we stop off at your place to continue this dispute? Which I will win."

So admirable was Margaret's offhandedness that Paul never suspected an ulterior motive in removing him back to his own apartment. The rain had stopped, but cabs were a rare commodity on Madison. Then magically, one was attracted to Margaret's outstretched hand.

"Couldn't you tell De Vere what you know and let him handle it officially?" Paul was desperate to find a way out of breaking into Harpennis House in the middle of the night.

"I'll tell him everything, once I'm sure, but just now I feel rather protective about the person or people who might be involved. I'm fond of De Vere, but I don't overrate his sensitivity in police matters. Then, too, I have no way of knowing what kind of officialdom might be assigned to the matter, if De Vere is busy with his other cases."

"All right," Paul said. "I'll consider asking her. Will that do for now?"

"Yes," Margaret said. She looked at her watch. "Where did this traffic come from?" The cab was inching downtown toward Chelsea. "It's getting late."


It was later than Margaret knew.

De Vere found a parking space close to the address Margaret had given him. He was certain he was making a mistake in entangling himself further with Lady Margaret Priam, but he had a weakness for fair, handsome women, however much he looked askance at the life-style this one represented.

He walked slowly toward Tenth Avenue. Substantial modern multistory apartment complexes stood on one side, older four- and five-story stone buildings on the other, now clearly no longer private homes but divided into apartments. The building he sought was a solid three-story house of gray stone with a sturdy front door leading to a tiny carpeted entranceway with three mailboxes. The name on apartment two read Dennis. He rang the bell. When the buzzer opened the second door into the building proper, he entered an intensely refined hallway with newly painted cream walls and dark moldings. A series of nineteenth-century prints in severe frames graced the wall above the carpeted stairway that rose upward.

"Darlin', is that you?" A honey-sweet voice floated down over the banister.

"Perhaps," De Vere said, not wanting to commit himself.

The glistening blond woman at the head of the stairs did not in the least resemble Margaret's description of a nice man, respectably employed, neither gay nor into drugs, although De Vere of all people was aware that things were not always what they seemed. This person was wearing a pale blue ultrasuede suit, deep blue suede boots, and large sapphire earrings.

"Why, you're not my boy!" Carolyn Sue Dennis Castrocani Hoopes said. "Stop or I'll call the police."

"I am not your boy, but I am the police," De Vere said. He showed her his shield.

"Oh, is he dead? Or what?"

"As far as I know, your boy is fine. Who is your boy?"

"Paul. My little Paul. I told Ben the city was no place for him. Has he done something terrible?"

"No," De Vere said wearily. "Not if he is Prince Paul Castrocani."

"That's him. Lord, but you gave me a fright. It's not easy bein' a mother."

"I should think not," De Vere said. "Let me explain."

By the time Margaret and Paul reached his apartment, Paul suspected that Margaret had something more on her mind than who had killed Mrs. Harpennis. He identified the other matter quickly when they walked into his living room and found his mother and Detective De Vere chatting cozily.

"Here he is. Come here, you sweet boy." Carolyn Sue threw her arms around Paul. "Lady Margaret, aren't you just the sliest old thing, fixing it up to have a policeman live here with him."

"Mother..." Paul began, and then turned around to look at Margaret, who wore a vague smile as though this were none of her affair.

"Ben will be so pleased," Paul's mother said. "He thinks lawmen are about the finest kind of human beings."

"De Vere," Paul said, "I want you to know that I did not encourage Margaret in this. It was entirely her idea."

"I believe you," De Vere said. "On the other hand, your mother has shown me around. There seems to be room for me, since my ex-wife took most of our common possessions. I work at odd hours, I don't think we'd get in each other's way. And the price is right."

"The price?" Paul's heard sank. The price was right for Paul, since it was nothing. His mother's trillions might make her think that nothing was also the right price for De Vere.

"I told Sam—" Paul's mother began.

"Sam?" Margaret and Paul spoke as one.

"I did tell you," De Vere said.

"I told Sam here that eight hundred a month and a share of the utilities sounded about right to me, but of course it's your business, Paul honey." Carolyn Sue winked at him behind De Vere's back.

"You are a princess, *mamma mia*," Paul said, "and a reader of my mind."

"There, that's settled," Carolyn Sue said. "Now I will not be a burden. I am only here until after poor dear Helene's funeral. I would not miss it for the world."

"Nor I," Margaret murmured. "Nor Paul."

"Well, then. We'll all go together. And Sam too."

"Perhaps officially," De Vere said. "Now I have work to attend to. Paul, after the funeral, we will discuss our arrangements."

"Why, we'll do that right now," Paul's mother said. "I'll

take us all to a nice little lunch and we'll settle everything."

"Thank you kindly, Carolyn, but I'm afraid I must decline," De Vere said firmly. "I will speak to Paul on Monday." He nodded to Margaret as he left, as if to say, The rich have lost this round.

So Margaret, Paul, and his mother went to a very expensive lunch at The Four Seasons, which Carolyn Sue ended up charging to some sort of platinum and diamond credit card. Paul's mother, in a rare show of restraint, did not mention the murder during the meal, although many illustrious society names from Manhattan to Dallas, Palm Beach to Monte Carlo did drop from her lips like so many dewy pearls.

# Chapter 14

"*Honey, that* was fine ol' lunch," Carolyn Sue said, "but now I have important things to do."

"Which are . . .?"

"Shopping of course. I want to get to Bendel's, although now that Gerry Stutz is gone, I simply don't know how it's going to survive. I brought two or three nice little black dresses with me for the funeral, but none of them is quite right. You understand." She appealed to Margaret, who naturally understood.

"Carolyn," Margaret said, "before you go, won't you tell us everything you know that might have anything to do with the murder?"

"I'm sure I don't know a thing," Paul's mother said. But she waved away a waiter who hovered. "Not having been there personally."

"Look," Margaret said, "besides what I've always heard about Helene, I've been hearing extravagant rumors about her past since it happened. From Poppy, from her maid, from Kasparian . . ."

"From Leila Parkins even," Paul said. "Leila's mother told her Robert's father wasn't. Someone else was."

Carolyn Sue laughed richly. "I ask you, what is a

rumor? Something everyone hears and talks about for a day. Then it becomes a fact, whether it's true or not. Nobody much mentions it again, and after forty years, it doesn't matter. Except if there is money involved, naturally."

"And the fact, true or not, in this case is?" Margaret leaned forward.

"Why, just what you said. Everyone used to say she had a string of boyfriends before she married de Bouvet. She was supposed to have been a fabulous beauty back then, long before my time. She had plenty of beaux right up until she married Nayland Harpennis. And no one could actually say who Robert's father was. There was all kinds of gossip about who did what to whom to produce Robert. I guess I heard all that about the time I first got to know Helene in the early sixties when I was just married and traveling around with Paul's daddy. Paul wasn't but a baby at the time. Robert was a teenager, a meanspirited boy. I don't know that she was still married to de Bouvet, but I do remember meeting him."

"He liked your style," Paul said. "Or so Mrs. Harpennis told me."

Carolyn Sue shook her head impatiently. "If you ask me, none of that's the least bit important. Who could possibly care? Robert got his piece of the inheritance when de Bouvet died. Helene went on to marry Nayland Harpennis and got richer, and picked up all those hangers-on like Basil Jones."

"What about Basil?" Paul asked suddenly. "He keeps suggesting that he remembers me as a boy."

"And he does," Carolyn Sue said. "Don't you remember when he came by the villa to visit your daddy? Trying to buy some ratty old thing or other we had around the place, pretending he was a collector. You must have been four or five. Cute as a button."

Paul closed his eyes. A damp, plump, and dusty man

knocks at the heavy carved door of the villa. Giuseppe, the old family servant, angrily shoos him away while Paolo peers around a crumbling corner of the house to see what is happening, and the bees hum in the hot Roman summer air. The man protests in slow Italian and waves a paper. Giuseppe reluctantly leads him into the house where Paolo knows his mother and father are resting in a cool white room in the back. The chipped fountain bubbles in the courtyard. Later, by the fountain, the man sits in the shade with Paolo and shows him shiny objects he says he has bought from people in the villas nearby.

"I remember him," Paul said. "He broke something valuable that day. Papa was furious. I remember now."

"He was. It was a very old piece of Venetian glass."

"He showed me . . . he showed me a ring," Paul said. "A lion's head, I think, that turned and opened, and there was a little space inside, where he said you could hide secrets. I think I didn't like him, and made myself forget him."

"Basil and his poison rings," Carolyn Sue said. "He went on and on about them. To prove to Aldo he was a serious collector, I suppose. He claimed the one with the lion's head had belonged to Cesare Borgia, but I never believed that. It was some kind of fake. People loved to see Basil comin'. They could get rid of all the old trash lying around by tellin' him it was the real Renaissance thing."

Carolyn was oblivious to the look that passed between Margaret and Paul at the mention of Basil's ring.

"I don't believe he has such a ring now," Margaret said carefully. "But then, I might not have noticed."

"He might have something similar," Paul paused and tried to visualize Basil's plump fingers gleaming with chunky golden bands. Or perhaps something with turquoise and diamonds.

"Or," Margaret continued with her own train of thought,

"he might have decided that it would be preferable to put such a ring aside for the present."

"Under the circumstances," Paul concluded.

"Aldo sold him a couple of seventeenth-century drawings that I know for a fact were done about 1925. Paul's own grandpa, the old principe, told me that." Carolyn Sue adjusted her sapphire earrings and looked at her Rolex. "Look what time it's gotten to be!" She stood up. "You two have a good time trying to pin Helene's poisoning on poor Basil who could have tipped the cyanide out of one of his precious poison rings into her dish. I can't imagine why he'd want to do that, but you two and the nice lawman can figure it out."

"We don't think Basil did it," Margaret said. "He had no reason."

"Except he hoped to be named a foundation trustee," Paul said. "Nina Parlons told me that. But Mrs. Harpennis at the ball didn't behave like a woman planning to entrust anything to Basil."

"I think it's right clever how well you play detective, darlin'," Carolyn said.

"Of course, Morley Manton also expected to be named a trustee," Paul said.

Paul's mother laughed merrily. "That's a better choice for murderer," she said. "Morley was around in the old days, too. He used another name then, when he was traipsing around Rome being kept by the old queens of both sexes. He was quite the boy then, but youth must have its fling." She touched her well-kept cheek to Paul's. "And, Paul honey, after you've finshed hanging Basil, why don't you catch up with me at Bulgari to look at the bijoux? I love to go shopping with a man, even when I'm payin'. If you come by Bulgari at four, I'll be having someone show me a few nice little things to take home. You take care of him for me, Margaret."

Carolyn Sue departed The Four Seasons like a woman intent on serious acquisitions.

"We must get into Harpennis House," Margaret said softly. "I'm sure Basil hid something in the office right after the murder. Janine must have found it and put it in one of those envelopes, but she didn't have the envelopes when I saw her leave Harpennis House."

"If it was a poison ring, the police should do the looking." Paul was firm. "I also believe it is illegal to prowl through buildings where one is not invited."

"Mmmm. Think of the winter debutante balls at which you will meet the richest and most eligible young ladies of the city. Leila Parkins's birthday party next month. She always invites me—and an escort, naturally."

"I don't believe you English are at all honorable people," Paul said glumly. "Why can't the police handle this?"

"Because I want to know first, before De Vere does," Margaret said. "Because he asked us to help, and only half meant it. We won't touch anything. Besides, they may have searched the house already."

"I don't want to get Basil Jones in trouble, no matter how distasteful he is."

"I think one has to do certain things ruthlessly when murder is involved," Margaret said. "Nina will give you the key if you are charming."

Max opened the door promptly for Margaret and Paul at Harpennis House.

"Nina is shut away," he said, "but I'll try to persuade her to make an appearance. Listen." Max lowered his voice to a silky whisper. "She's really hiding out. There are things going on here today she doesn't want to get involved in. Miss Sheridan is upstairs in the library with the foundation lawyers and the accountants, and I can't begin to tell you who else. Mrs. Harpennis's son and his wife. Such dreadful things they're saying. People taking money from the foundation, and I don't know what all."

Nina jumped when Max pushed open her office door and Paul and Margaret entered.

"Oh, it's only you," she said. "Help."

"What's going on?" Margaret asked. "More murders?"

"No. It's money, and who was paid what for what. Nothing much to do with the ball, but plenty to do with the Youth. Janine is panicked. Apparently she okayed invoices or didn't or Helene did." Then Nina smiled faintly. "I believe it has something to do with Morley. Unnatural acts were mentioned in passing. The usual things."

"Ah, Morley. A number of things seem to have to do with Morley." Margaret and Paul exchanged a look, then Margaret nudged Paul forward into his mission.

"Nina, could I speak privately?" Paul dripped with charm. "I need to ask a favor." He glanced toward her office.

If Nina had any thought of resisting, she did not reveal it.

"Well, yes. Of course," Nina murmured.

Scarcely was the door closed behind them than Margaret started to slip down the hall toward the grand staircase.

"My turn to eavesdrop, sweetie," she said without turning around. Max, emerging from the shadows, stopped in his tracks. She glanced over her shoulder at him. "You'll stay put right here, and sound an alarm if anyone else starts up the stairs."

"I will," Max said. His gaze was admiring.

She tiptoed across the polished expanse of the ballroom. Someone had drawn the drapes across the tall windows, bringing the room to late dusk. Margaret could not now remember exactly where the table where Helene had died had been placed. The doors to the library were slightly open, and a sliver of artificial light shot across the polished floor. The words from behind the door were indistinct but the tone spoke volumes. Deep lawyerish voices, calm and sensible, droned on, punctuated by Janine's weary, tearful voice. Sara offered shrill interjections. Robert uttered semi-Gallic chirps. Margaret drew closer.

"These irregularities will naturally be thoroughly investigated. We have every intention of uncovering the truth about the allegations that have come to our attention. Before her death, Mrs. Harpennis informed us of information she had received, and the accountants have since discovered certain irregularities."

"I suspected! I told! I made every effort to . . ." Janine sounded hysterical. "Basil and I tried to tell Helene."

*"Mon Dieu!"*

"Your Lord is not the question here, Robert. Your inheritance is." Sara had a practical streak to her. "We want nothing to delay the transfer of your mother's money into your hands."

There was a very long silence.

Someone cleared his throat. "Madame de Bouvet," said a voice belonging to the American legal profession at its high-priced best, "do not labor under any delusions about the nature of your husband's inheritance. This is not the time or place to discuss it, but be assured that you and M. de Bouvet are not here as Mrs. Harpennis's heirs. Indeed, I must tell you that except for a modest bequest to you, the bulk of her fortune remains with the foundation. We asked you here as individuals who might shed light on other matters. Matters you might have heard about from the late Mrs. Harpennis. We wish to clarify certain allegations."

There was another long pause, and Margaret wondered if Robert and Sara had lapsed into comas at the news that the millions on which their expectations had rested had perhaps been designated to flow elsewhere.

The voice spoke again. "We are trying to determine informally, without involving the police at this time, whether Miss Sheridan, Mr. Manton, and/or Mr. Jones were engaged in schemes to defraud the Harpennis Foundation. Or if they were aware that this might be taking place. Miss Sheridan claims that Mr. Manton was so engaged. Mr. Jones has denied any such activity, although he says he suspected something of the sort."

"Nonsense," Janine said sharply. "I informed him. I hinted to Mrs. Harpennis. I told the police."

"Did you indeed?" said the lawyer. "This comes as news to me. Did my colleagues have any knowledge . . .?"

There was a hum of denials.

"I told them anonymously," Janine said. "Publicity is bad for the foundation."

"Have you proof then?"

"Yes, I want proof," Sara interrupted the lawyer. That would cost an extra thousand on the billing, Margaret was sure. Lawyers did not take kindly to civilian interference.

"I have proof of many things," Janine said. "But I will not be badgered. If Mr. Harpennis were alive today, he would not allow you to harass me."

"We are not harassing you, Miss Sheridan." It was a different, but still legal voice. Soothing, it was, and reasonable. "We, like you, want only what is best for the foundation. It must continue to be a monument to philanthropy."

"You understand," Janine said. "Others do not realize how important the foundation is. They tried to tear it down, and I struggled to keep it up. I did everything I could."

"I'm sure you did." Still soothing.

"This woman is an idiot." Sara sounded vicious.

"How dare you." Janine sounded like righteousness outraged. "If you knew the shocking truth about your precious Robert—"

"Shut up!" Sara was shrieking, something she was good at.

"Ladies . . ." A third lawyer spoke.

Margaret almost expired when a hand touched her shoulder. Max quickly put his finger to his lips and mouthed "Basil Jones," then pointed downstairs. He beckoned her to follow him toward the stairs. Margaret was torn between staying and leaving. She hoped Janine had run out of things to say.

"He's in his office," Max said. "He didn't see me, but he slipped in and locked the door behind him. I heard him opening drawers and things, so I came to get you. Your friend the prince left, but he said to tell you that the mission was achieved. You're to meet him at Trump Tower in the atrium. He said that is close to the Pierre and Bulgari. I just love all of this."

"Please, Max. It's serious."

"I mean Bulgari and all that." He looked back at her, hurt, as he preceded her down the stairs. "Listen!" He stopped. There were sounds from the office Janine and Basil shared. "He's still there. What will we do?"

"I'll just have a word with him," Margaret said. "It doesn't concern you. Is Nina about?"

"She went out with the prince, but said she'd be back. They're an adorable couple, don't you think?"

"As long as she doesn't love him for his money," Margaret said absently.

The door to Janine's office was locked. Margaret knocked gently. "Basil, it's Lady Margaret. I must speak to you."

"Can't."

"Of course you can. It will only take a minute."

Basil opened the door a crack. Behind him Margaret could see a desk with drawers opened recklessly and papers strewn about.

"I am looking for some personal property that I mislaid. Janine left a message that it was safe." Basil looked guilty.

"I merely wanted to warn you that Janine is upstairs

with the foundation lawyers and the de Bouvets. I didn't think you'd want to become involved."

Basil patted the perspiration on his forehead. "I don't. You are a friend, Lady Margaret. In the library? It was the next place... It is the place where Janine likes to hold meetings."

"I believe she is accusing Morley of something."

"Stealing. And a ghastly past. I personally have known all about him for twenty-five years since I was buying... buying pieces for my collections in Italy. Then Janine managed to find out everything. Stupidly, we never came right out and told Helene, and look what has happened. I must leave before they come down, mustn't I? I'll just put things back in order..."

He closed the door quickly, and Margaret heard the key turn.

Margaret was thoughtful as she left Harpennis House. There were things hidden in the old, unfriendly house that would clear up some matters relating to the murder. If Paul had actually gotten the key from Nina, they would find them tonight.

One part of her argued that her plan was dangerous and probably illegal. Another part, more determined and foolhardy, declared that it was perfectly all right. She couldn't allow De Vere and the police to shake up the lives of innocent people whose names could make unfortunate headlines. It was the least she could do for her friends and her class. A third part of her mind openly confessed that she wanted to show De Vere what she was made of.

# Chapter 15

*Park Avenue* slopes south from the East Sixties, ending with the golden-tipped Helmsley Building at Forty-Sixth Street. The constant traffic that flows along it in both directions seems somehow to be more refined than on other Manhattan avenues. There seems, overall, to be a better class of automobile on Park.

Margaret decided to walk a few blocks along Park before she turned down a cross street toward Fifth Avenue to meet Paul and plan the evening.

Manhattan being full of the poor and homeless importuning the prosperous (although admittedly it was a rare occurrence on Park Avenue), she barely registered the soft whisper, "Excuse me."

Margaret shook her head and proceeded on without looking at the source.

"Please, Lady Margaret."

Belle Nagy, of all people, had rested a heavy bag on the hood of a parked car and was fumbling with an umbrella to ward off the showers that were beginning again.

"Mrs. Nagy, what on earth?"

"I took the subway to Grand Central," Belle said. "I am on my way to the House to pick up something from Miss

Sheridan, and then I will walk over to Helene's apartment to pay my respects. I have not been able to reach Robert at all."

"He's seeing lawyers at Harpennis House," Margaret said. "He's likely to be tied up for some time." Mrs. Nagy didn't need to face Sara enraged by the thought that the Harpennis wealth had slipped through her hands. "Let's duck in over there for tea. I was hoping to have a chat with you, in any event." The Mayfair Regent was half a block away. What matter that the price of tea was geared to ruling families and stock-market manipulators and not to working aristocrats and elderly widows.

"I thought perhaps Miss Sheridan would be at Harpennis House today, but no one else." Belle allowed herself to be led.

"It's brimming with people," Margaret said.

"And I have to see Robert," Belle said.

"No," Margaret said. "I believe you should leave it for now."

"There are things he needs to settle," Belle said, "now that Helene is gone. Things he must know."

"It can wait," Margaret said gently. "Robert is really very involved with serious foundation matters. Sara is there, and Miss Sheridan. And the lawyers, naturally."

The richly subdued interior of the hotel enfolded them. Margaret nodded to the concierge, who had raised an eyebrow at Belle's crammed shopping bag (even though it did carry the name of Bloomingdale's). They found a quiet corner sheltered by a flower arrangement that could be had for the price of a small car. Margaret poured tea.

"You are very kind, Lady Margaret," Belle said. "I've been fortunate all my life in having kind people look after me. Helene tried to be kind, but money and power change a person, don't you think?" Belle gazed at middle distance and seemed to be seeing old times unfolding once more.

"You knew each other for a long time," Margaret began.

"So long," Belle said. "I was always a shadow to her sunlight, even when we were schoolgirls. So popular and pretty she was. They were not well off. I used to let Helene borrow my dresses and bows. I remember she took a lovely blue dress my mother had only just bought me. . . ." Belle shook her head. "I shouldn't dwell on the past. I always promised Istvan I wouldn't think about it."

"It's understandable," Margaret said. "You've lost an old and dear friend."

"I sometimes try to balance what I gave her with what she gave back. The richer she became, the more trivial the crumbs, but the more she asked. Ah well, thanks to her I have managed to see places in the world I never dreamed of back in Ohio."

"There, you see? She was kind to you."

"But you're wrong. She was cruel to everyone who took trouble for her," Belle said with odd serenity. "Mr. Jones is one who knows that very well. He was so loyal, and she made promises she had no intention of keeping. Miss Sheridan was made dreadfully unhappy by her. At least Robert will have Helene's money, and the power of the foundation. He will have what is rightfully his."

"Oh, I don't think so," Margaret said carefully, since Belle seemed as convinced as Sara that the Harpennis millions would be Robert's. "The lawyers were quite clear in stating that Helene's money would go elsewhere. I mean to say, I overheard them say that Robert should not expect to inherit the Harpennis money."

Belle stared at Margaret. "But that isn't right. I don't understand."

"Neither do I," Margaret said, and regretted that she had mentioned it. "Perhaps I misheard what was said."

"No," Belle said softly. "That would be like her. I wonder how I can find out for certain."

"Perhaps you should be in touch with Poppy Dill. She

seems to know everything. She's probably dug up the will by now."

"Everything. I wonder. I have to go now." Belle fumbled to slip into her coat and catch the handles of her shopping bag.

"Mrs. Nagy, wait." Margaret stood up, too.

"No, please. There are things I must do. Thank you so much for the tea. You are too kind. Too kind." Belle Nagy put out her hand, frail and veined, an old woman's hand with carefully polished pink nails, a slendar tasteful gold bangle bracelet, a lacy cuff at her wrist. Genteelly shabby, sad and dignified.

Where would she go? Margaret wondered, that poor, sad remnant of Helene Harpennis's life. Surely not to Harpennis House, into the den that harbored the fearsome Sara, the lawyers, and Robert.

Robert had remained a shadow throughout this dreadful affair, with Sara acting the role of Lady Macbeth with gusto. If he were not de Bouvet's son, was he indeed Istvan Nagy's son? Was that the shocking truth Janine had mentioned?

As her suspicions mounted, Margaret told herself she was getting like those women who lived on gossip when they would be better off with red meat. Some days she got no satisfaction from being a part of the world they inhabited.

She finished her tea and thought back over years of her own memories. The lush summers of her childhood in England, safe and cosseted by family and servants. Schoolgirl adventures. The party life of London nights, the garden party days. Horses and hunting and the subtle pursuit of eligible young men. All in all, a safe cocoon constructed of position and financial security. How different from the roots Helene and Belle and the others had arisen from to find a place in society.

And who had killed Helene Harpennis? Society, to be

sure. The social web of dependency and envy, too much money or too little. Love and hate. Pride and revenge.

Margaret went off to find Paul, uneasy because she sensed she was beginning to understand why the fateful hand had been raised against Helene, and whose hand it was.


Poppy Dill liked to feel that she could doze on Saturday afternoons without feeling guilty about not reading press releases, society magazines, letters from friends and their enemies around the world.

This Saturday afternoon she kept half an ear awake for the telephone call she was expecting. In between patches of light sleep, Poppy traced out what she recalled of Helene's history from back in the days before the Second World War. Helene had made a vivid splash in the social waters of New York, coming from nowhere and fascinating a good many likely lads in the nightclubs and at fancy dances.

Helene in London in the frantic prewar days, in France before it fell. Married to de Bouvet, who was never as rich as people believed. Helene back in the States, and when the Germans had been defeated, back in France, to end an unhappy marriage. Eventually among the lovers and admirers, she achieved the status and wealth she had been seeking in the person of Nayland Harpennis.

"De Bouvet was a peasant with a fairly good tailor," Helene had once told her. "If you only knew what I had to do to survive with him."

Poppy had nodded sympathetically. Naturally she knew. It was her business to know.

The phone rang.

"Hello? Yes. I've been waiting for your call."

Poppy's legman had done his work.

"No fortune for the son," he said. "Does that surprise you?"

"No," Poppy said. "Go on."

"No foundation position for the son. No trusteeship for Jones, Manton, or anyone else that I recognize. The name Charles Stark does get mentioned. He seems to be the heir apparent as far as heading the foundation goes. A modest legacy to a Mrs. Belle Nagy, also Jones. Almost everything stays with the foundation. Did I do good?"

"Fine," Poppy said. "Just fine. Charlie Stark is perfect. Do you suppose Robert or anyone else knew about her will?"

"I don't think so. It wasn't easy for me to find out. People might know it now, after the fact of murder. Do you know who did it?" Poppy's young newspaper friend sounded eager.

"Perhaps," Poppy said. "I have someone coming here on Sunday with concrete proof. Justice will be done."

Justice? Poppy considered that. Perhaps she meant justification. It didn't matter. It was her big journalistic moment. She took up a lined pad and a sharpened pencil.

*Today's moving farewell to the late Helene Harpennis was capped by bringing her killer to justice. In an exclusive interview, this reporter learned from the lips of . . .*

The pencil slipped from Poppy's aged fingers, and she dozed again.

"Darlin', these are just the most adorable little trinkets, don't you think?" Carolyn Sue slipped a huge gold bracelet studded with indecently large emeralds onto her wrist.

"You do not wear green," Paul said severely.

"I do," Carolyn said, "when I want to."

Paul fingered the copy of the key to the back entrance to Harpennis House resting in his pocket. At least Nina had been obliging about the key, although she had taken back the original he had copied with a firm statement that she would deny knowledge of everything. Happily she had chosen not to accompany him to Bulgari, where he might have been expected to purchase a token of his thanks. He would take her out someplace very nice and expensive once things were more settled.

A salesperson, effusively attentive to the needs of Mrs. Benton Hoopes, nevertheless remained vigilant lest she thoughtlessly slip a forty-thousand-dollar bauble into her ample Ferragamo handbag. Carolyn Sue was picking over a tray of diamond bracelets. The emeralds had been restored to their case.

"Sweet, I call it," Carolyn said. She held up a circle of diamonds with a single large sapphire. "Now you know I do wear blue. I'll take it," she said to the salesperson. "No, don't wrap it. I'll wear it."

"*Carissima mamma*, it is dangerous to carry jewels about the streets of New York." Paul was appalled to see the amount the salesperson was writing up on the sales slip.

"Honey, if you can't afford to lose it, you can't afford to own it," Carolyn said.

"It's not the bracelet," Paul said. "Rather it is your life that I am concerned about."

"Don't you worry," she said. "Isn't it just the sweetest little ol' thing?" She held out her wrist where the diamond circle glinted and the sapphire was a brilliant blot of blue.

"Very nice," Paul said, and looked at the bracelet thoughtfully. "Very nice indeed."

Paul sent his mother home with her outrageously expensive souvenir of New York before she could do more damage. He rejected two cabs. One was driven by a dark-browed Arab whom Paul judged to be a PLO terrorist. The other was some type of Oriental who did not appear to understand English and might have been uncertain of the city he was in. Paul settled on a gruff but genuine New

Yorker. Abe Feldman assured Paul that he knew where the West Twenties were, that he lived in Brooklyn and all three of his children were in college. Abe didn't seem surprised that a curriculum vitae was necessary for a five-dollar taxi ride.

"My mother is from Texas," Paul explained.

"You can't be too careful nowadays," Abe said.

"I'll make you a nice dinner," Carolyn said as she settled into the cab.

Abe Feldman inserted his taxi into Fifth Avenue traffic and sped away downtown. Paul felt that possibly his mother and the many thousands of dollars in precious stones adorning her would reach the apartment safely.

Dinner was likely to be the result of Carolyn Sue's foray into his neighborhood deli. When she was slumming with him in Chelsea, she took special delight in the little white plastic containers of potato salad and olives, the chopped chicken liver and the sliced pastrami and turkey breast. Bagels and bialys. A large half-sour pickle.

Margaret was waiting for him in the atrium of Trump Tower, gazing upward at the expanses of orange marble and the humming escalators. The fountains gushed and re-cycled, to the delight of tourists visiting shops they could never afford in this life, while the occasional bag lady slipped by the flamboyantly uniformed doorman to breathe purified air.

"Do you have the key?" Margaret demanded.

He handed it to her.

"Good," she said, "and don't think that just because you've given it to me, I'm going to let you out of coming with me tonight."

"It was not easy to find a locksmith on Park Avenue," he said. "There are none. I found one between boutiques on Madison."

"I hope it works."

Paul hoped it did not.

"We should meet on the corner near Harpennis House latish . . . ten-thirty? The streets should be quiet."

"Margaret, I don't think . . ."

In her stern look, he saw his visions of twenty-year-old heiresses to half of South America vanishing back into distant pampas. "All right. But listen, my mother has bought a bracelet. A thin circle of diamonds with a large sapphire."

"How nice," she said absently. "I think we only need to look at the offices and the ballroom and library upstairs. The house must have sixty rooms, but I doubt if the upper floors are used at all. Wait. A bracelet—of course! How clever of you. But I don't remember . . . It is something to think about."

"We should not spend a long time in the house." Paul was feeling nervous already.

"Half an hour, ducky, and it's off to the clubs. Leila is certain to be out on the town. We'll make the rounds, and if we don't find her, there are others just as much to your taste."

## Chapter 16

*Standing in* the shadows across the street from the back entrance to Harpennis House, Paul felt his deli dinner lying heavy on his stomach. It might be the corned beef his mother had served with the potato salad, but it might equally well be nerves.

Carolyn Sue had left early to go out to friends who had just acquired four upper floors of 100 United Nations Plaza, complete with swimming pool, indoor formal garden (plus croquet lawn), and twenty-five rooms, none of them decorated by Morley Manton.

"Maybe not quite four floors," Carolyn Sue said, "but enough space for a Texas gal. They put together the party just for me. I hope Barbara Walters can make it. The Petries are out of town, I understand, and Brooke Astor is so terribly busy these days."

Margaret had promised to be prompt, but she was already ten minutes late. It was chilly, even though Paul had donned what he hoped was a suitable housebreaking outfit: black trousers, heavy black sweater, and black Reeboks with unobtrusive silver trim.

A few cars turned down the street from Park and headed toward Madison—a Mercedes, then a Jaguar and a gleaming Rolls, a few nondescript cars, a delivery truck heading home. A figure hunched over against the September dampness rounded the corner and paused near the Harpennis House alley gate to light a cigarette. Paul tensed. A stray mugger knocking off from a hard day's work or merely a late-night stroller? Another delivery truck sped by and blocked Paul's view of the alley. It screeched to a stop at the red light at Madison. The potential mugger had disappeared.

Paul stepped out of the shadows and edged cautiously along the buildings to the corner of Park. There was no sign of Margaret on foot, or of a taxi dropping her off.

Paul turned north and walked past the front door of Harpennis House to the next corner. The tall, dark ballroom windows reflected the lights from the buildings across Park Avenue. Still no Margaret. Paul waited on the corner, under the concealed and vigilant eye of a uniformed doorman in the foyer of the corner luxury apartment building.

Within Harpennis House, there was stealthy movement. A drawer in the office of Janine Sheridan was opened by a gloved hand, the contents examined and rejected. Other drawers were opened as the search grew more frantic. At a sound outside the office door the searcher froze, then withdrew into a dark corner and waited.

The footsteps in the hall were faint but not hesitant. Someone stopped at the office door and rattled the knob, but it was locked. The footsteps moved on, and the silent searcher breathed in relief.

On the basement level, so quietly that no sound was heard, a person slipped through the door from the alley into the musty old kitchen where the antique iron range, deep rusty sinks, and a jumble of worn tables and chairs told the history of a dead past. Ghosts of Irish maids and irascible, plump cooks glided there; the imported butler sadly recalling his former situations with truly aristocratic masters; stern housekeepers keeping watch over their domain.

The new arrival found without hesitation a narrow door that opened onto the back stairs. Carefully, quietly, the intruder followed the long flights of stairs all the way upward to the garrets where the housemaids of the past slept after wearying days, far above the glittering rooms of the rich and powerful inhabitants of the house.

Once again the door from the alley edged open. This visitor walked up the stairs to the white room that was now the gallery, into the marble hallway, past the offices to the grand sweeping staircase, and began to ascend.

Cautiously, a tiny sharp light from a flashlight guided the way up the stairs, a polished banister to the left, smooth white walls to the right.

The sound of movement from above halted the upward progress. The light was switched off, but the person continued step-by-step toward the second-floor ballroom.

Yet another person slipped through the alley door, found the way to the back stairs easily, and opened the door onto the ballroom floor. There was a shaded light on in the little library off the ballroom and the sound of a search.

On the topmost floor, Eduardo Cruz extracted a well-wrapped package from inside his leather jacket and placed it behind a shutter on a window that looked down on Park Avenue. Then he slipped back through the door to the servants' stairs and made his way quickly toward the basement.

At the ballroom floor, he stopped and listened. He turned the knob slowly and pushed the door open an inch. He peered into the darkness, saw the sliver of light beneath the closed library doors. He opened the door wider and saw a figure gliding across the ballroom floor, and then another edging along the walls.

A voice from the darkness whispered, "Who's there?"

There was no answer. Eduardo watched the two move silently across the ballroom and one by one enter a far room. He listened for voices when they discovered each other, but there was no sound. Then he detected movement at the top of the stairs. Another was in the house. Eduardo quickly closed the door. This was no place for him, or any wise person.

The kitchen, at least, was empty except for its ghosts. Eduardo shook his head. This was bad business, and he didn't want to be part of it. A package deposited in Harpennis House from time to time for Morley Manton was one thing. Eduardo never asked what it contained, although he had his suspicions. But the murder of an old woman and these crazy people roaming around in the darkness were more than he had bargined for.

They are all mad, he thought. These rich people are all lunatics. He hurried toward the security of New York City's streets, where at least the dangers were predictable. As he reached the alley door, he stopped.

More people, more whispers in the dark. Eduardo sighed and stepped into a dark alcove. Someone was fumbling at the lock.

"It's open!" The voice was far too loud for the circumstances, not American and definitely female.

"Hush, Margaret, please." A man spoke.

"No one's around, Paul, but why is the door unlocked?"

"Either the caterer forgot to lock it when his men left, or there is someone around. Please be quiet."

"I have a torch," Margaret said, and switched it on. Paul grabbed it from her hand and turned it off.

"You are not good at clandestine housebreaking," he said. "Let us draw on my knowledge of intrusion into the homes of attractive young women for purposes of assignation. A light is not a good idea. Come after me."

In the brief flash of light, Eduardo recognized the lady, blond and slim, seen at the ball. The one he had danced with.

"Miss . . ."

The voice out of the darkness stopped Margaret and Paul.

It occurred to Margaret that a proper response was a scream, but she thought better of it.

"Who's there?" she said.

"You would not know me," Eduardo said. He stepped out of the alcove.

"But I do," she said. "You danced with me at the ball. A Youth."

"I know nothing of the old lady's death," he said. "I am here on other business."

"We do not ask what it is," Paul said.

"There are people here." Eduardo spoke slowly, to give himself time to decide whether to make a break for the alley or keep these two from whatever madness was occurring upstairs.

"Who?" Margaret and Paul spoke together.

"How many?" Margaret wanted to know.

"I do not know who," Eduardo said. "There are three or four, perhaps more. Walking about in the dark, suspecting the presence of the others, but they did not come together. Ah!"

Eduardo took Margaret's arm and pulled her into the alcove. "Come," he hissed to Paul, who did not hesitate.

A person emerged from the dark kitchen and headed toward the door, found it open, and left the house.

"That's one." Margaret found her mouth effectively shut by a large hand.

"*Por favor*, miss. Shut up." Eduardo was tense. "One of these people is a killer. You do not wish to be the one who stops him."

Another came from the shadows, cautiously opened the basement door, and departed.

"Are there more?" Margaret managed to whisper.

"*Sí*."

"Is there a way for us to leave?" Paul whispered. "Now?"

"Señor, this is like the Puerto Rico Day parade," Eduardo said. "Next come the floats with the beautiful girls."

They all instinctively looked upward at a noise deep within the house. Too loud.

Someone ran past them, hunched over, fumbled at the door, and left. It wasn't possible to tell if it was male or female. Then there was silence. A long, frightening silence.

"Wait here," Eduardo said. "You don't know the ways of this house as I do. Wait." The last was spoken emphatically, as though he understood that one had to be firm with the likes of Margaret. He glided away into the dim reaches of the kitchen.

"What is going on?" Margaret whispered. "I attempt a minor detecting effort, and the entire world is here before me."

"There are secrets to hide or discover," Paul said.

Margaret shivered. "I feel things moving," she said. "Small things at my feet."

"Merely mice," Paul said. "It is the large moving beings that should worry you. Ah."

Eduardo had returned. The collar of his leather jacket was turned up and his chin was sunk into his chest. He looked worried. "This is your problem, man," he said. "It is very bad business. I am going home. You never saw me, I don't know you."

"Absolutely," Paul said. "We should go as well."

"No." Margaret was firm.

"Miss, there is trouble up there."

"What kind of trouble?"

"Death," Eduardo said. "If you wish to see it, take those stairs up to the white room and the big hallway."

He was gone, into the alley and up the cement steps two at a time.

Margaret was already on her way up to the gallery, with her flashlight showing the way.

Paul said, "What did he mean by 'death'?"

Margaret, ahead of him, said, "I judge he is quite literal in his statements."

Death was waiting for them in the marble entrance hall. Margaret's flashlight picked out the dark shape on the white floor. She flashed the light on the walls and located a switch. Suddenly the hallway was ablaze with light from the hanging chandelier.

"Janine!" Margaret knelt beside the ugly sprawled body and fumbled to feel for a pulse. "Call an ambulance, quickly." But as she spoke, she felt no sign of life.

Paul did move quickly, rattling the locked doors of the offices, then remembered the pay phone in the coatroom that Leila had mentioned.

"I think she was hit from behind." Margaret was looking at her hand streaked with blood. "Maybe if help comes soon . . ."

Paul had already disappeared into the coatroom.

Margaret froze at a sound from above. She stood and glanced upward toward the dark upper floor.

Slowly she started to climb the stairs. She reached the entrance to the ballroom, where she and Paul had stood the night of Helene's murder, and looked into the blackness. She saw no human form, sensed no movement.

I am doing something terribly stupid, she thought, but I am not afraid. Whoever is about is merely one of the people I dine and drink and dance with at charity balls and cocktail parties. Someone like me.

She took a cautious step forward into the darkness.

Another step.

The blow that fell on her missed her head and struck her shoulder. She stumbled and fell to her knees. Someone rushed away, and Margaret heard a door slam. Then she heard a telephone ringing on the floor below.

A stab of pain in her shoulder caused her to gasp and kneel for a moment longer. Suddenly Paul bounded up the stairs.

"What happened?" He knelt beside her.

"Someone hit me. Gone, down the back stairs."

"Are you hurt?"

"No." She stood up. "Not much."

Paul turned the flashlight on a tall brass candlestick on the floor.

"I rang 911. Miss Sheridan is certainly no longer alive. Then I called my mother." He looked a little sheepish. "She required me to carry the number of the home she is visiting. She called De Vere. For some reason, she had his number. Then she rang me back. He is coming."

"Amazing what your mother is capable of. De Vere? He will be furious." Margaret rubbed her shoulder. Then she said, "Quickly. Let's look around, before they get here. But don't touch anything. Clues and fingerprints, you know."

"Now you worry about clues. What do we look for? Where?"

"The library," Margaret said, and headed across the ballroom.

In the library, the curtains had been closed. A small lamp beside a leather sofa was still lighted. A candlestick that matched the one Margaret had been struck with stood on a table. Leather-bound volumes had been swept off the shelves and lay scattered across the rich oriental rug. Drawers in the dark mahogany end tables had been riffled and left open. The coromandel screen that had protected Helene Harpennis in death was pushed against one of the ceiling-high bookcases.

"This is a room where nothing was kept except books that no one read," Margaret said. "No one used this room.

Therefore, I surmise that someone was looking for something that had been put here recently and temporarily. How does that sound?"

"It sounds like trouble for us," Paul said gloomily.

"It sounds to me as though Janine hid those envelopes I saw her with in the library and came back to get them tonight. But someone else wanted them badly."

"Basil?" Now that it had come to this, Paul did not like to speak his name.

"Or Robert and Sara? The shocking truth Janine claimed she had."

"One of them killed her to get the envelopes, has them, and has departed." Paul wished they, too, could depart.

"Well, there is nothing near her body."

"Except," Paul said, "the police. I hear them. Let us go downstairs and stand full of innocence and tearful grief."

"Excellent idea. Wait." She stooped had picked up a small object half-hidden under the sofa. It was a 35-mm transparency, which she held to the light.

"A tropical statement," she murmured. "If I am not mistaken, it is a photo of an Istvan Nagy painting. So Belle did leave photos with Helene, and Janine was hiding them, too. Interesting." She slipped it into her pocket. "I think we could leave the Adjuvant Youth out of all this," she said as they descended the stairs. "I don't think that young man is a killer."

"Not a killer of old women in stately mansions," Paul said.

"I'm glad of that," Margaret said. "He is a divine dancer."

# Chapter 17

*B*y the time De Vere arrived, there were uniformed police in abundance, ambulance personnel, a medical examiner, a homicide detective, and general confusion. - 

"This is illegal," De Vere said to Margaret as he strode into the hallway and frowned: first at her, then Paul, and finally the body of Janine Sheridan around which a crowd of official persons had gathered. A short, ill-tempered man whose ancestors Paul had mentally placed somewhere south of Rome, most likely Naples, called minions down from the ballroom floor where they were doubtless digging up clues.

"Lieutenant Rossi is not going to be as kind to you as your previous experience with the police might have led you to expect," De Vere said. "When I asked for your help in a minor way, I did not mean housebreaking and murder."

"We had a key," Margaret said.

"The door was unlocked in any case," Paul said.

De Vere glared at him. "You deserve worse than you'll get. Suppose you tell me first why you decided to break in here."

"We wanted to find out some things," Margaret said. "We thought we'd look around."

"You couldn't let the police do the looking?"

"We thought they—you—probably had."

"For a variety of reasons, we had not. Even law enforcement is sometimes subject to pressures from various quarters. Mrs. Harpennis had powerful friends. I don't know the details, and thankfully, I am not in charge here tonight."

"Then why are you here?" Margaret asked.

"Paul's infinitely sensible mother suggested I provide some quiet support. Besides, I didn't want you to face . . ."

He stopped. Paul saw the look that passed between them. He was philosophical about it. Even if he lost Margaret's multitude of connections to the world of single and well-off young women, he might at least become free of the necessity of investigating murders and harboring a police detective in his apartment.

"Thank you," Margaret said.

"Now," De Vere said, "I am curious to know why the Social Register decided to gather here tonight. You people are dangerous to be around—two old women dead in the space of three days."

"There were quite a lot of people in the house tonight," Paul said. "Someone killed Miss Sheridan, as you see, and then attacked Margaret."

"What!"

"It's nothing," Margaret said. "Not lethal, merely a sore shoulder."

"Exactly who was here?"

"We don't know," Margaret said quickly. "It was dark. Three, maybe four. And the Youth."

Paul's expression clearly reminded her she wasn't to mention the Youth. De Vere's expression demanded an explanation.

"A boy I danced with at the ball. Tall, good-looking. He was here on . . . other business."

"Cruz? Eduardo Cruz?"

"I don't know. I'm sorry we got involved in this, De Vere. We were only trying to help."

De Vere's stern expression softened. "I know, I know. But Lieutenant Rossi will not be so understanding. He takes homicidal activity among the upper classes even more seriously than I do. Did Cruz happen to mention Morley Manton?"

"Not that I recall," Margaret said. "Did he, Paul?"

"I believe not," Paul said. He was busily calculating whether his Italian blood would serve him in good stead with Lieutenant Rossi, or whether the traditional hostile feelings between Romans and Neapolitans carried over to American shores.

"The visitors tonight—three or four, I think you said— was one of them Manton?"

"No. He's so tall, we would have recognized him."

At that moment, as Janine Sheridan's body was removed via the front door, a uniformed policeman appeared from the back of the house with the just-mentioned Morley Manton, who was bristling with fury.

"I demand . . ." he said in a very loud voice.

The policeman placed him in front of Lieutenant Rossi, who looked up at Manton and said a few quiet but firm words. De Vere joined them and listened.

"He was found entering the alley door," De Vere reported back to Margaret and Paul. "He claimed that he had left something important here which he needed desperately at"—De Vere looked at his watch—"close to midnight."

Morley spotted them and strode over to them.

"Lady Margaret, Prince Paul, what is this all about?"

"Janine Sheridan is dead," Margaret said. "Likely murdered."

"Good Lord! But it has nothing to do with me."

"Not obviously, not any more than Mrs. Harpennis's death did," De Vere said.

Morley turned pale under his technologically induced tan. "I had nothing to do with either death," he said.

"It's not for me to say who's under suspicion," De Vere said. "But you must be aware that your activities have been under scrutiny by certain authorities."

"And the foundation," Margaret added, then bit her lip at a frown from De Vere.

"I don't know what you mean." Morley Manton sounded uncharacteristically defensive.

"I think you do." De Vere was made cheerful by the sight of Morley's discomfiture. "You'll be hearing from me—after Lieutenant Rossi has had his time with you." He turned to Margaret. "And with you two. Please don't be as obstructive with him as you are with me. Just give him the truth. I'll stick around to take you home."

"How kind," Margaret said coldly.

Paul watched De Vere take Margaret's arm and lead her firmly to the other side of the marble hallway. He leaned forward so that their heads were close together. Then Margaret smiled at something he said and nodded. He touched her cheek, a small, intimate gesture that the watching Paul noted seemed to please her. He sent her back to Paul.

"What an interesting man," Margaret said. "I believe he quite likes me."

"I judge you are correct," Paul said, "but what kind of trouble are we in? I see my dinner invitations turning to ashes."

"We are not to worry. Mr. Rossi will be very cross with us, but we have probably done nothing wrong." She felt the transparency in her pocket. "Nothing seriously wrong."

The butler at the Harpennis apartment informed a policeman who called about the time that Margaret and Paul were facing the wrath of Lieutenant Rossi that the de Bouvets had been out for the evening to dine with acquaintances. They had returned a short time before and had retired.

"I shall certainly inform them that you telephoned," the butler said, a bit too sharply. He did not appreciate being roused once he himself had settled in for the night. "And that you expect to call on them tomorrow."

He did not report to the police that behind the closed doors of the bedroom occupied by Robert and Sara were the sounds of furious argument. Since it was being conducted in a combination of French and English, he trusted Claire, hovering outside the door in her plain dark robe, to catch the full flavor and import of the discussion and convey it to him in the morning.

What Claire heard was that since Robert's miserable old nag of a mother had not left her immense fortune to him, Sara was finished with the marriage.

"Legal recourse?" Sara screamed at Robert's mumbled words. "You won't have a chance to contest the will if we don't destroy those damned documents. Now someone else has them, and don't pull that '*ma cherie*' crap on me. Since you won't do anything, I'll find out something from someone who knows."

Claire decided that as soon as the funeral was over on Monday, she would depart this place. Because the butler had always been civil to her, Claire knocked on his door before returning to bed and suggested that he consider his own future sooner rather than later.

Poppy Dill slept fitfully, now and then surfacing to catch a few minutes of the movie playing on the VCR atop her television set. *High Society*, dear Princess Grace's last film. How greatly she was still missed in international society.

Poppy was cross when her phone rang so late, and then

she was wide-awake. It was Margaret, telling her about Janine.

"She was coming here tomorrow," Poppy said. "She said she had important proof relating to Helene's murder."

"If she had proof, it's gone now," Margaret said. "I think I know who must have killed them both. Poppy, what do you know about Robert de Bouvet? Really know, I mean?"

Poppy did not reply for a long time. Then she said, "Nothing I can prove absolutely. Janine was going to show me . . . Well, now that she's gone, I'll have to try other avenues. If you do know something, will you give me an exclusive?" The shades of Dorothy Kilgallen and Adela Rogers St. John hovered at her shoulder.

"The most exclusive," Margaret said. "But I want you to promise one thing. Don't see anyone tomorrow. Don't let anyone in. Promise me. I don't want any harm to come to you."

"I can't think why anyone would harm me, and I'm not in the least worried," intrepid Poppy said, but she promised. "Can you come here after the service and talk over everything?"

"Yes," Margaret said. "After our good-byes to Helene."

Poppy immediately called Basil. "Janine has been murdered."

"How . . . how terrible." His voice was high-pitched and strained. "I have been here all evening working on my little article on Renaissance medals," he added although Poppy hadn't asked.

"I do believe you, Basil," Poppy said. "And I can't have you here to lunch tomorrow as we planned. Something has come up. We'll meet at Helene's funeral."

After Poppy's call, Basil Jones sat in his apartment in the dark and tried to control his fit of trembling and terror. Everything had gone wrong. His ring was nowhere to be found, although Janine had promised it was safe. Someone had it. All that trouble, and nothing to show for it.

Basil looked into his future and was frightened by what he saw.

Belle Nagy made herself a glass of warm milk and retired to her bed. How old she felt; how wearying the day had been. It seemed that she had walked miles and miles. Even from the other side of life, Helene was using her.

Tomorrow, she would reach Robert finally. He could not refuse to see her, nor would she allow the butler to rebuff her at the door as he had that afternoon.

Tomorrow she would try again. Robert and that woman he had married might now be very glad to see her.

Morley Manton, released by the police with warnings not to leave town, made plans to do just that. He wrote a note to be sent around to Poppy, saying he could not after all accompany her to Helene's funeral. Then he placed a few quiet phone calls to acquaintances at various locations around the world where it might be possible to escape impending unpleasantness.

"Flight to escape prosecution" had an unfortunate sound to it, but Morley thought it best to be prepared. He had always been fond of Morocco, but he wasn't certain if it held some kind of extradition treaty with the United States.

Eduardo Cruz decided that it had been some time since he had seen his big sister. That she happened to live in Fajardo, on the east coast of Puerto Rico, was mere chance. It was certainly a considerable distance from Spanish Harlem and the Adjuvant Youth.

In any event, Eduardo sensed that the future of Adjuvant Youth was not promising.

Carolyn Sue Hoopes, high above Manhattan in the sinfully luxurious triplex her New York friends called home, was resplendent in a brand-new Valentino evening frock that had set her back six thousand dollars. As the guests sipped after-dinner drinks, Carolyn was able to create a really delightful momentary stir with the news that Janine Sheridan had also been murdered. No one cared in the least about Janine, but Helene's death was revived as a delicious conversational topic.

"Mark my words," a distinguished former assistant secretary of state remarked. "It won't do anyone any good to find out who did it. It will expose a lot of dirty linen that doesn't need to be aired."

"I never liked that son of hers," someone else said. "And not simply because I find the French so difficult."

"French? Him? By upbringing only," someone else said. "You remember the stories. My mother knew all about it."

"All of that is ancient history," the hostess said.

Then an impending scandal that involved adultery, elopement, divorce, and some expensive settlements to keep everything quiet captured everyone's interest.

"So much more amusing than those Wall Street people going to jail," Carolyn Sue said. "I knew they were too perfect a couple for it to be true."

"I agree," said the hostess of the evening. "Let me tell you what I heard about him from . . ."

The ladies put their well-coiffed heads together, and the death of Helene Harpennis was forgotten.

* * *

At the end of a long night, De Vere hustled Paul into a cab with a command to go straight home and keep out of locked houses.

"The house was not locked," Paul said for the hundredth time, but De Vere was not listening.

"Ring me tomorrow, Paul," Margaret said. Then De Vere took her away, and Paul retreated to the safety of his apartment.

"The Starks have asked us to lunch on Sunday," said the note on Paul's bed, written in his mother's endearingly immature hand. Rudiments of education were all that were needed by rich Texas girls. Carolyn Sue's wisdom, such as it was, had been acquired through life experience. Paul definitely did not want to get up on Sunday to lunch with the Starks.

He placed the note from his mother on the bedside table and fell into deep sleep and heavenly dreams in which Leila Parkins figured, along with a row of tanned, naked female bodies on a Mediterranean beach under clear skies.

When he awoke finally in late morning, he found his mother looking through the ads in the Sunday *New York Times* and drinking coffee from a cardboard cup.

"You've been to the deli already," he said.

"I love those boys," Carolyn Sue said. "Greeks. I used to think Jewish people ran Jewish delis in New York, but you see what a wonderful place this city is. Chris, Nick, and George. Lovely boys. From Piraeus. I brought some coffee for you—" She waved her hand toward the kitchen. On her wrist flashed the new diamond bracelet that could support Chris, Nick, and George for several years.

"About the Starks," Paul began. "I don't think . . ."

"I told them we'd be there at one. You'll never guess who's visiting them."

"Dianne's sister?"

"How did you ever know?"

"I sensed the possibility. I must telephone Margaret."

Margaret answered on the first ring. "Well, love. How are you after our rousing night?"

"At least I am not in jail. My stepfather would not approve of that. How are you?"

"The shoulder is tender. De Vere was solicitous and annoyed by turns. We worked it out."

"I am sure you did," Paul murmured. "My mother and I have been asked to lunch with the Starks. The sister is here."

"No. Really? That was quick work on Dianne's part."

"I don't want to go."

"You must. Charlie Stark could be useful. He might take you away from that job you hate. Dianne is certainly good-looking. The sister might not be at all bad."

"In any case, I do not intend to do any detecting today," Paul said firmly. "I need my rest."

"As do I," Margaret said. "And I have to leave almost at once for lunch out on Long Island in Locust Valley, and be back in the city for a dinner being given for Eddie Kenmore, who's here from England."

"I do not know Eddie," Paul said.

"No," Margaret said. "You wouldn't. He's a duke. But we do have urgent business Monday morning before the funeral."

"Yes?" Paul said cautiously. He had hoped that somehow he could fail to attend the funeral and please his employers at United National by showing up there. "I ought to be at my job."

"Nonsense. Simply everybody will be at the funeral. They can't expect you to miss it."

"We will again be helping the police?" he asked with resignation.

"Something like that. We're going to Queens."

"Queens? Who is that?"

"What, not who. The borough across the East River. Sort of like Brooklyn, only different."

"I see. Why?"

"I want to speak with Belle Nagy. I have tried to reach her today, but she appears to be out. In any case, it will be better face-to-face. We will bring her to Manhattan for the funeral. We'll need to meet early. About eight-thirty or quarter to nine. In front of the United Nations building. You come uptown, I'll come down."

"All right. I will meet you, if you feel I am needed."

"You might be," Margaret said. "By the way, in the event that you are concerned, De Vere is still much taken with the idea of moving into your place. Provided you cease being a detective. After the funeral."

"I will be pleased to be relieved of the responsibility."

# Chapter 18

*At eight*-forty-five on Monday morning, the United Nations building at First Avenue and Forty-Fifth Street was not yet thronged with tourists. Margaret was waiting for Paul at the locked gates to the visitors' entrance. Across the East River, a giant Pepsi-Cola sign kept watch on the deliberations of nations.

"What did you think of Dianne's sister?" They settled into a taxi and headed toward the Queens Midtown Tunnel.

Paul grinned. "*Bella. Bellissima*! Why do these young American women I meet look so *uniformly* attractive? I know some quite rich people in Europe who are definitely ugly."

"It's all that lovely milk they're given when they're children and plastic surgeons and spas and diets when they grow up."

The taxi deposited them on Vernon Boulevard in Long Island City, in the borough of Queens.

"This is not a pleasant part of the world," Paul said when he surveyed the neighborhood, "but again, it is no less pleasant than some quarters of Rome." He looked at the drab, unprepossessing storefronts. Activity on a modest scale was afoot. Schoolchildren were on the sidewalks, herded by anxious mothers toward a school bus stop. An old man with a wobbling, fat dog huffing behind him strolled on the opposite side of the street. Corner stores sold coffee and newspapers. A blare of rock music issued from a dilapidated car that rounded a corner and raced by. The three- and four-story brick buildings that housed the area's residents were not at all grand.

"It is a long way from Park Avenue," he said.

"Not a very long way at all," Margaret said. "Look."

She walked him a few yards along the sidewalk and pointed west, through an empty lot between two buildings. The Manhattan skyline was a postcard view: the silver Art Deco spire of the Chrysler Building, the shining slab of the United Nations, the familiar Empire State Building, with clusters of glass-walled office buildings and terraced apartment houses.

"And soon enough Park Avenue will move to this side of the river and steal that view from the present inhabitants." Margaret cast one backward look at the skyline and said, "Belle's building should be right around here." She compared a building number to an address noted on a slip of paper. "Here it is."

The little entrance hall to the four-story building was swept but shabby. Eight mailboxes had hand-printed names in the slots. The last one read NAGY. 4B. Margaret pushed the bell and peered into the hall through the heavy glass pane.

"I have followed you without question," Paul said, "but could you not tell me why I will have to climb four flights of stairs to see Mrs. Nagy?"

"I think I can get some answers. About Robert. About the past. Why someone might want to kill Helene and Janine." She pushed the bell again. "Look." She handed Paul the transparency she had picked up at Harpennis House. "I found it Saturday night in the library. I showed it to Kasparian, and he hawed and hemmed and then said it was an

Istvan Nagy painting certainly, because no one in his right mind would try to imitate that style. I wondered if Belle had been there, and if she had seen anything but was afraid to tell the authorities."

"She doesn't appear to be in." Paul was hopeful that they could leave quietly. "Perhaps she went early to the funeral."

Margaret fumbled in her purse. "You're supposed to be able to open a door with a credit card. This door looks ripe for..."

"No! There are people here." Paul grabbed the American Express Gold Card from her hand. "We escaped incarceration or worse on Saturday on the legal technicality that the door was already open. I do not wish to tempt fate."

Margaret snatched the card back. "Kasparian is sending a precious bit of Chinese antiquity to Paris next month. He asked if I knew someone who could be trusted to act as courier. Strong, young, reliable, presentable. All expenses paid. I was thinking of suggesting you."

"I submit," Paul said. "But for your part, remember that De Vere would not like to hear about this venture."

"A standoff," Margaret said, and slipped the card gently between the door and the frame. The door opened. "How simple!" She pulled Paul into the dim hallway and shut the door behind them.

"How illegal."

"We're not robbing anyone," Margaret said. "Come along."

The steps upward were carpeted with a worn, patterned runner. By the time they reached the second floor, Paul was breathing heavily. He made a mental note to suggest that his mother invest in a health club membership for him.

"I wonder where Mrs. Nagy could be," Margaret said.

"Perhaps the slayer of old women has sought her out." Paul stopped, shocked at what he had offhandedly said.

"You don't suppose . . .? You could not reach her yesterday, she does not answer now."

"I think not," Margaret said with less confidence than she felt. "I hope not. Only two more flights."

The lighting seemed dimmer the higher they ascended. On each narrow landing there were doors to two apartments. Paul thought he heard faint sounds of a television program from one. A dog yapped behind another door and was silenced by a woman's sharp voice. Those who went out to work had already departed. On the top floor, a dusty skylight let in a little more light. On the wall between the two apartment doors hung a painting of a sturdy workman in an undershirt with the Queensboro Bridge behind him.

"A Nagy," Margaret murmured. "His socialist period, I judge." She pressed a bell embedded in the door of 4B beneath a peephole. Then she knocked.

"Not here." Margaret said. "We must get inside." She stooped and looked under the straw doormat. "Try the ledge above the door. In an old neighborhood like this, people often . . ."

"You are looking for the key. You cannot do this."

"*We*, you mean. It might be important." Margaret was firm.

Paul ran his hand along the lintel. "Nothing." He was relieved.

"Too bad. No. Wait."

She walked to the painting, lifted it slightly out from the wall, and ran her hand along the bottom and sides. "Aha!" She fumbled at the lower left-hand corner and extracted a key that had been attached to the back of the painting with black electrician's tape. "Here we are."

She inserted the key into the lock of Belle Nagy's door and turned it. The lock clicked open.

"I merely want to look around," Margaret said. "You can wait outside if you wish. I won't touch a thing. I just want to be sure nothing is wrong."

Margaret edged into the apartment. "Mrs. Nagy?" Margaret's well-bred voice rang through the apartment. "Is anyone home?"

The apartment was spacious but old. The dark wood floor was polished to a gloss and the sturdy furniture in the living room looked as though it had existed forever and would last decades.

The windows looked out on the magnificent view they had seen from the street. There was, as far as they could tell, no hideous crumpled body lying anywhere on the floor.

"Wait." Paul felt a stab of fear. Something in the apartment was moving. "Someone is here," he whispered.

Margaret laughed. "It's a cat, look."

Belle's Silver walked stiffly from another room and sat down before them. He watched them gravely as Margaret walked through the apartment, touching nothing and observing everything. The wicker sewing basket beside an armchair. A pile of back issues of *Art in America*. Many— too many—paintings on the walls. Overlarge for the room, glaring colors, many styles, all Nagys. Margaret held up the transparency she had found and matched it to a huge painting that seemed to show palm trees and ocean, although the colors were quite remarkable.

"The tropical statement," Margaret said.

A studio portrait photo of a fierce, handsome, heavyset man with bristling eyebrows, so ethnically Hungarian it was undoubtedly Nagy himself. A photograph of Robert. The young Helene against a background of hills covered with vineyards. Another photo: an enlarged snapshot of Helene and Belle flanking Nagy, with a scrawny child who could only be Robert in front of them. Nagy was smiling down at Helene, not his wife. A formal wedding photo of Robert and Sara in a regal wedding gown.

"Curious," Margaret murmured. "Have you caught on that people imply Nagy was Robert's father?"

"Nagy? But Mrs. Nagy was a friend." Then Paul sighed. "I believe these people capable of any behavior."

Margaret was looking at a scrawl on a pad beside the phone. Poppy Dill's telephone number and her address. Margaret thought a moment, and then dialed Poppy.

"I know you're busy dressing, but have people been calling you?" she asked when Poppy answered. "Yes. I see. *Sara* called? What on earth for? Both Belle and Basil? Listen, Poppy, Paul and I will be at the church early. I want you to sit with us. Please take care."

When she hung up, Margaret was thoughtful. "A good many people seem to believe Poppy's reputation—someone who knows secrets nobody else knows, and is in a position to announce them to the world. She wouldn't tell me what they think she knows." Margaret paused to open a polished wooden box on the sideboard.

"Margaret, we cannot stay..."

But Margaret was prodding the contents of the box. "Aha."

Paul caught her slipping something into her pocket. "Margaret, you have taken something. You said you would not."

"It's nothing important. Really. Let me have a look..."

Margaret opened a door and found herself in the studio where Nagy had worked decades before. Unfinished canvases leaned against the walls, brushes stood in cans, tins of pigment in a row, bottles containing chemicals, an array of mat knives, a palette with the memory of colors long ago laid on canvas, stretchers, linseed oil, varnish. It was all dusted and neat. While Paul fidgeted nervously under the curious and unswerving gaze of the cat, Margaret examined everything in the studio.

"Come, Margaret. There is nothing to find here."

"There is," Margaret said from the studio. She emerged with a frown. "But by someone other than us."

She looked into the kitchen. A dish of cat food, fresh

and moist, was on the floor near the refrigerator. Belle had indeed departed early, leaving plenty of food for the cat. "I think we ought to hurry back to Manhattan," she said.

She locked the front door behind them and replaced the key behind the painting in the hall. Paul was convinced they would never reach the street undetected, and his relief was enormous as they left the building. Margaret scanned the streets, but no taxis appeared to cruise Long Island City. Finally a passing youth directed them to a subway entrance. "Takes you to Grand Central, then to Times Square," he said. "No taxis around here."

"I know Grand Central," Margaret said as they waited in the grimy station with a dozen resigned riders for a train to carry them under the river to Manhattan. "I have taken a train from there to Greenwich, in Connecticut. The church is only a few blocks up Park Avenue."

After what seemed a long time, a train rattled into the station. It was crowded with people who did not seem to notice that there were too many of them. Margaret and Paul managed to squeeze in. Margaret freed her arm to see her wristwatch. "It's after ten already, but this ought to be a very brief ride."

"What have we accomplished?" Paul asked, and grabbed an overhead strap to steady himself. He did not like the look of the black youth leaning against the door. The train lurched and slowed down, and someone jammed an elbow in his back.

"A little," Margaret said. "I think we can keep further damage from being done if we arrive at the funeral early enough."

"For what reason?"

"To notice who goes in, and more important, who goes out with whom. I especially want to stay with Poppy, who will probably be mobbed. Everyone who was at the ball will be there."

Paul said, "I hope I do not encounter Countess Cloissoné." Then he said suddenly. "Why does the train appear to have stopped moving?" They were stopped in the tunnel, with no friendly lights of a station in sight.

"Damn," Margaret said. "I don't want to be late."

"You'll be late," said a voice behind them. "The trains have been screwed up all morning." He was a portly businessman who overcame his native reluctance to make eye contact with a fellow rider and looked Margaret over appreciatively.

Several unintelligible sentences were spoken over the train's loudspeaker.

"There's a train stuck somewhere up ahead, and it's blocking all the trains behind it," the businessman said. "At least this car isn't crowded."

To Paul, who always rode buses in preference to the subways, it seemed frighteningly full of people either resigned to their fate or singling out victims for attack.

"At least the problem isn't a fire on the tracks," the businessman told Margaret reassuringly. "Or a derailment. It will be all right."

"I hope so." Margaret began to fidget. "It's more or less a matter of life and death. Murder actually."

The businessman eyed her warily. "I see," he said, and buried himself in his *New York Times*.

After several tense minutes, the train lurched and shuddered, and moved ahead a few yards. Margaret's sigh of relief came too soon. The throb of the motor died and the car plunged into darkness, except for scattered, weak emergency lights. The groan from the riders sounded ugly.

"If we do not reach the church in time for the service itself," Margaret said, "we will surely be there by the time it ends. Nothing could happen during a funeral."

"Nothing could happen during a ball attended by a great many distinguished people," Paul said, "but it did."

After endless minutes, the lights came on and the motor started. The train moved slowly ahead. Too slowly for

Margaret since her watch told her that Helene's obsequies were about to begin. The next time the train halted, the voice on the loudspaker informed them that only the first car of the train had managed to enter the station at Grand Central and would move no further for the time being. Riders in the rear cars could make their way through the train from car to car to exit at the front.

"Come on," Margaret said. "We may yet be in time." She was the first to push open the heavy sliding door and step across the coupling to the next car. "I don't want another murder."

Paul followed and admired the skill with which Margaret forged ahead through the riders funneling through the narrow doors from car to car.

"So sorry." She elbowed a little old lady out of the way. "Emergency, you know."

Paul struggled to keep up with her.

He heard her say to a tall young Sikh in a turban, "I'll just squeeze by, shall I? Lovely." She turned around to signal to Paul to hurry. "Not much time. Come *along*."

He rather rudely ploughed through the crowded cars after Margaret and wondered who she thought would be murdered this time.

## Chapter 19

*The parade* of limousines arriving for Helene Harpennis's last social engagement necessitated a contingent of police to direct traffic in front of St. Bartholomew's church on Park Avenue. Curious midmorning passersby—the messenger boys on their bikes, tourists emerging from the Waldorf, executives on their way to offices from lengthy power breakfasts or on their way out for an early lunch, cruising cab drivers, and the aimless, the homeless, the truant students—paused long enough to stare, in the hopes of seeing a celebrity or two.

"Is that the mayor?" someone asked. A mild cheer, scattered boos.

"It is," another said. "Doesn't miss a trick."

Shut out from his desired role as First Mourner, Basil was all gravity and grief, and dressed with great care. He hovered at the top of the shallow steps near the great carved doors of the church. He watched alert chauffeurs leap from driver's seats to open doors and allow affluent society ladies in glorious black to emerge and totter up the steps on life-threatening high heels.

"Ah . . ." A sigh from the onlookers at the sight of a local television news anchorperson, a Broadway star, the social senator. Ambassador Duckworth arrived, among many serious men with expensive haircuts and newly barbered chins. Countess Cloissoné had chosen navy instead of black. Her hat was fabulous. The Brazilian beauty who had sambaed as Helene had her fateful encounter with the sorbet paused at the top of the steps and showed a flare of red taffeta petticoat.

Paul's mother had arranged a limousine for herself ("One likes to keep up appearances, even in New York") and alighted in time to witness the rare spectacle of Poppy Dill by daylight in the open air. Naturally someone had loaned her a limousine. She looked quite elegant in her antique Chanel with a little hat perched on her head and a wisp of veiling across her forehead.

Basil started down the steps to Poppy but was forestalled by Carolyn Sue, who commandeered Poppy and accompanied her up the steps. Their heads were together as they crammed in all the gossip they could manage of the past few days or decades.

De Vere stood near the entrance of the church and observed it all. He especially admired the way Leila Parkins undulated toward the steps in a satiny deep gray suit. She had very nice legs. He remembered seeing her at Morley's party. Morley himself slunk in, speaking to no one. He had chosen not to take wing for other hemispheres. Mrs. Nagy was almost invisible amid the solemn glamour of the occasion.

Carolyn Sue finally handed Poppy over to Basil and looked about for Paul and Margaret. She settled for De Vere.

"I can't imagine what's become of them," she said. "Paul went off somewhere with Margaret early this morning. Detecting."

De Vere winced. "I hope not."

"Look. Robert and Sara," Carolyn Sue murmured, and noted Sara's impenetrable black veils. "If she's hiding tears, they're tears of pure rage. Paul heard Helene cut them off without a penny."

"So I have been informed."

"It would be a pity if Robert murdered his mother for money and the effort was wasted. Listen, Sam. I don't know if it's important, but Poppy Dill just told me confidentially she's about to get her biggest story ever. Someone who knows everything about the two murders phoned her up and is going to meet her to tell her all. She wouldn't say who. Is that wise?"

"The gossip lady," De Vere said. "She just went into the church with Basil Jones, right? I'll keep an eye on her. Paul didn't mention where he and Margaret were going?"

"Not a word. I hope they won't be late."

"You go in," De Vere said. "I'll wait until the last minute for them." He scanned the stragglers entering the church but did not see Margaret. Carolyn Sue adjusted her diamond earrings and ascended the steps.

Poppy and Basil were seated together, with an empty space on either side of them. By some silent consensus, the mourners seemed to imply that to sit near Basil might be harmful to one's reputation, in the event he'd done something foolish. On the other hand, since Poppy was entirely above suspicion, not having been at the hall at all, one or two people made their way down the aisle to have a word with her.

As the service undertook to enumerate Helene Harpennis's virtues in the Here, and her possibilities in the Hereafter, Margaret and Paul reached the car that had nosed into the subway station beneath Grand Central.

As Charles Stark spoke a eulogy that was both short and appropriate, Margaret and Paul emerged from the depths of the subway and sprinted through Grand Central Station, scattering derelicts and commuters in their wake.

As the organ produced tasteful, dignified music to inspire Helene's mourners to a contemplation of the transitory nature of life even in the highest social circles, Margaret and Paul dashed through the Pan Am Building out onto Forty-Fifth Street and into the gilded, carpeted Helmsley Building to reach Forty-Sixth Street and Park Avenue.

For a group of people whose attention span was notoriously short, the assembled company at Helene's funeral service did not get restless until near the end. Then the nervous coughs began, the rustle of taffeta, the stifled yawns, and the shifting movements that signified that well-bred bottoms were seeking greater comfort. The officiating cleric forged ahead against the rising tide of boredom.

Margaret cursed the very high heels she had chosen to wear and gallantly trotted ahead up Park toward the church.

When the service ended, society as Helene Harpennis had known it stood up and shook off its stupor, ready to find their limousines and gossip somewhere pleasant about who wore what and who would be wearing what to the next gala event.

The aisles were clogged with the departing, who had done their solemn duty and now greeted friends they hadn't seen since the day before.

*"Darling, how sad it is, but you look perfectly divine."*

*"Did you catch what the son's wife was wearing?"*

*"I loathe funerals. Where are you lunching?"*

*"We don't have to do anything ghastly like go to the house and eat casseroles, do we?"* The last betrayed a small-town upbringing the speaker thought she had long ago smothered.

*"Trust Helene to end in a cloud of scandal. The dignified thing would have been something terminal, but not unsightly."*

Margaret and Paul came to rest, out of breath, at the corner of Fiftieth and Park and surveyed the triple-parked cars waiting to receive their passengers.

With a most unladylike show of force, Margaret pressed through the throng in the hopes of finding Poppy and seeing her home. She was touched to see that Kasparian had come to pay his last respects. Carolyn Sue emerged like the star she was.

"Did you see Poppy?" Margaret asked her breathlessly.

"Well, you made it. A lovely, lovely service."

"Poppy," Margaret repeated. "I must find her."

"I should think so," Carolyn Sue said. "She's planning to sneak off to interview the murderer or somebody. De Vere promised to look out for her."

"Good." Margaret was relieved. "Paul, look inside the church and locate De Vere and Poppy. Carolyn Sue, see if you can track her down in case they left."

Paul's mother obliged with a cheery, "Ooo-hoo, Charlie, Dianne, darlin'. Did y'all notice Poppy leaving?"

Dianne Stark shook her head. Margaret looked frantically for any of the logical suspects but found none. Poppy herself was nowhere in sight.

Charles Stark said, "I believe I saw her getting into a limo. There might have been someone with her."

Paul emerged from the church with his bevy of beauties: Leila, Nina, and Dianne's sister vied for his attention. He grinned sheepishly at Margaret. "No Poppy," he said. "De Vere can't find her. Leila thinks she was one of the first to depart."

"Lord, but he's just like his daddy," Carolyn Sue murmured. "Look at him and his women. Irresistible."

"This is serious," Margaret said. "If Poppy didn't leave with De Vere, there's no time to waste. I have to get to her."

Carolyn Sue had a practical plan. "Take my limo and go to Poppy's apartment. Paul and I will keep looking here and catch up with you." She scanned the row of waiting cars. "Damn, but these limos all look the same." She tripped down the steps and accosted several uniformed drivers.

Margaret shifted impatiently.

Carolyn Sue waved. "Found the right one," she said, and spoke to the driver. "Honey, can y'all drive this thing fast through traffic? Real fast, I mean."

"Yeah," he said. "Fast getaways used to be my specialty, but the traffic today. . . ."

"Life or death, and I'll make it worth your while."

Margaret got into the limo. "She means it. And I do need to get uptown terribly quickly."

The driver shrugged. "I can try," he said. "I'm sorta out of practice. Say, is that guy on the steps waving at you? Looks like a cop to me."

"He is," Margaret said. "Let him find his own limo."

The car shot out into the traffic on Park Avenue going north and wove through the lanes of traffic, slipping through yellow lights as they blinked to red. It seemed an interminable ride. New York traffic had no respect for the overriding importance of speeding stretch limousines.

When they finally rolled up in the short curving drive in front of Poppy's apartment building, Margaret was out of the car before the driver could open her door. "Wait here for Mrs. Hoopes. Tell her to follow me in." She walked quickly into Poppy's building.

"Poppy Dill is expecting me," she said to the doorman before he could demand her name. He fell silent before her grim determination.

In the elevator, Margaret fidgeted. She should have spoken to De Vere and told him what she'd found out. She should have told him what she suspected and what she knew. What Janine probably knew, and Poppy as well.

The door to Poppy's apartment was open. Margaret dashed into the marble foyer. She could hear Poppy's voice from her boudoir down the short hallway from the living room. It did not sound as though she were interviewing someone with an eye to the front page.

"I know. I mean, I've always suspected." Poppy's voice rang with a touch of panic. "But I've never told, I never would."

Margaret flung open the door to Poppy's boudoir and didn't hesitate. She grabbed Belle Nagy's upraised arm as Belle struck out at Poppy with a mat knife of the sort Margaret had seen in Nagy's studio. Poppy clutched a satin pillow to her bosom, frail defense against the lethal-looking blade. Margaret held on, although Belle struggled with unexpected strength.

"Belle," Margaret said desperately. "Please don't."

"She wanted to write it up for the newspaper," Belle said in a low, vicious voice. Suddenly her strength ebbed, and she sagged. Margaret took the knife from her hand.

"She told me it was a big story," Belle said. "But I thought if no one else knew, Robert could still contest the will."

Poppy straightened her suit jacket and brushed back a lock of hair. She seemed to have recovered quickly from her moment of terror. "I could have helped you, Belle. The power of the press. Only Janine knew Helene kept the secret well."

"I knew, too, finally," Margaret said. "Starting with a hint from Helene's maid."

Carolyn Sue burst into the room, Paul right behind her. "Sit down, Poppy honey. It's okay now."

Paul eyed the knife in Margaret's hand. "You should have had me with you," he said gallantly.

"Stupidly, I wanted to do it all myself."

Carolyn Sue turned to Margaret. "Then suppose you tell us—"

"Yes," De Vere said at the door. "Suppose you tell us all." He did not sound pleased, and he looked furious. Behind him, Robert de Bouvet stared openmouthed at the scene.

"But I do not understand," Robert said.

"You haven't understood anything since time began," Sara said, and brushed past him. "What the hell is going on?"

"Robert," Belle said softly. "It was all for your sake."

"This dumb cop *forced* us to come here," Sara said. "He claims Robert was at Harpennis House on Saturday, when that Sheridan woman was killed." Then she was silenced by a look from Robert that promised further mayhem if she did not cease.

"Belle," Robert said gently. "You cannot mean that it was you who performed those terrible acts, and in my name. You have been almost like a second mother to me."

Belle smiled faintly. She seemed exhausted. "Indeed, Robert. Indeed I am your mother." She bent down, picked up her handbag, and took out a packet of yellowing documents. "Helene was here during the war when you were born, and de Bouvet was in France. She begged us to let her take you, so he would have the heir she couldn't give him. He would believe you were his son, she said. She promised she would take care of you, better than we could, and we agreed. She never kept promises, and I thought if she were dead, you would have . . . everything. So I slipped the poison into the sorbet. I found out too late that you were to have nothing."

"And Janine?" Poppy asked, ignoring De Vere's strangled groan at her inteference in this pressing police matter.

"She had these papers," Belle said simply. "I needed them."

Then Belle bowed her head and refused to say anything more.


"Belle poisoned Helene?" Paul said. "But how? And where would she find cyanide?" He glanced over his shoulder to where De Vere was moodily standing guard over Belle, awaiting a police woman. Poppy and Carolyn Sue had retired to the living room. Sara had been banished from the apartment, but Robert sat beside Belle and held her hand.

"She picked it up from the materials Nagy supposedly used for creating pigments," Margaret said. "Some of them are quite dangerous. Arsenic in emerald green, cyanide in Prussian blue. I recalled something about that from my art studies, and Kasparian reminded me more exactly. Then I saw the chemicals and things in Nagy's studio. They were fairly new. I guess she replaced them regularly. I think she believed he would come back. She must have carried the cyanide along to the ball, convinced that Helene would break her promise about the Nagy show. Which she did."

"You should have told De Vere," Paul said.

"I would have, at the funeral, but there wasn't time. He's terribly angry with me, don't you think?"

Paul nodded. "I judge he is angry with you because you put yourself in danger. And he is generally displeased with all of us interfering civilians."

"Then I shouldn't show him this just now," Margaret said. "It was in Belle's apartment." She held out a thin bracelet, with turquoise and clear stones. "Not real diamonds, I'm afraid. When I found the bracelet Nina had noticed, I knew for certain."

# Postscript: After the Ball Is Over

*P*oppy Dill, flushed with success from her big story centered on her brave interview with a murderer, nevertheless still sent her "Social Scene" column down to the newspaper every day at noon:

> *Social New York is delighted to see that ravishing young couple, Prince Paul Castrocani and Nina Parlons, simply everywhere together. They met at the Harpennis Ball, which was the tragic setting for . . .*

Margaret tore out the page of the paper that contained Poppy's column and handed it to Paul, who was stretched on a sofa in his own living room with memories of murder receding rapidly.

"I told you Nina was a lovely girl," Margaret said. "You make a very nice couple. Better than Dianne's sister, who's too innocent, or Leila, who definitely is not."

"What you and my mother did not tell me was that Nina's family owns most of the Pacific Northwest."

"I didn't know that," Margaret said, "but naturally your mother would. It's the kind of thing she's best at."

"Unfortunately," Paul said gloomily, "no matter how

215

rich she is, she's not willing to settle down with me. She says she's looking for someone more . . . substantial."

De Vere picked up the newspaper page and read:

> . . . *Last week, Paul and Nina attended an intimate brunch hosted by Lady Margaret Priam for Paul's mother, Mrs. Benton Hoopes (the former Princess Castrocani), who was returning to her fabulous Dallas home. Charles Stark and his adorable wife Dianne were among the guests, along with S. Langley De Vere (one of Lady Margaret's many beaux).*

"I made up the name," De Vere said. "Poppy needed something snappy. Do you have a great many beaux?"

"Quite a few," Margaret said. "But not as many as Paul has lady friends. Do you like living here at Paul's place?"

"As long as Paul understands that I play detective and he plays prince."

"But Margaret is the one you should be saying that to," Paul said. "I am the innocent bystander always. Besides, in two weeks I leave for Paris, thanks to Kasparian, and you will have to look after Margaret. But I warn you: she will try to bribe you to do things against your better judgement."

"I will remember that," De Vere said. He did not seem displeased by the prospect.

# About the Author

JOYCE CHRISTMAS has written seven other novels: *Hidden Assets* (with Jon Peterson), *Blood Child*, *Dark Tide*, *A Fête Worse Than Death*, *Simply to Die For*, *A Stunning Way to Die*, and *Friend or Faux* as well as several nonfiction books and children's plays. In addition, she has spent a number of years as a book and magazine editor. She lives in a part of New York City where as yet Society rarely sets foot.